COVERT COFFEE

Natalie Buske Thomas

ISBN: 0-9666919-7-0

DEDICATION

To Brent, Cassandra, Nicholas and Savannah

Special Thanks To

Lita, Julie, Jay, Kelly, Joy, and Jama for backing the
Covert Coffee oil painting book cover project

AUTHOR'S WORKS

GENE PLAY *Serena Wilcox Mystery 1*
VIRTUAL MEMORIES *Serena Wilcox Mystery 2*
CAMP CONVICTION *Serena Wilcox Mystery 3*
THE MAGIC CAMERA *Juvenile fiction*
THE SERENA WILCOX MYSTERIES: BOOKS 1, 2 & 3
ANGELS MARK *Serena Wilcox Mystery 4*
FRED BORN GIFTED: RESOURCE GUIDE TO THE
GIFTED AND DIFFERENTLY WIRED *Non-fiction*
COVERT COFFEE *Serena Wilcox Mystery 5*
BLUEBIRD FLOWN *Serena Wilcox Mystery 6*
Contributing author to the following titles:
CONFESSIONS OF SHAMELESS SELF-PROMOTERS,
CONFESSIONS OF SHAMELESS INTERNET
PROMOTERS, THE OBVIOUS EXPERT, A SECOND
HELPING OF MURDER
Plays, Adaptations and indie movies:
A CHRISTMAS DEED, THE MAGIC CAMERA,
PILGRIM'S PROGRESS: CHRISTIANA'S STORY,
NARNIA: THE SILVER CHAIR, WALK THE PLANK,
JONAH'S LUCK
Oil paintings:
SAVANNAH READING IN THE BUTTERFLY GARDEN
traveling exhibit with EASEL for 14 months
LIFE SUSTAINING *Women and Water Rights juried exhibit*
RON AND JOY BEFORE THE WAR *Touched by War
exhibit*
COVERT COFFEE *Oil painting COVERT COFFEE book cover*

www.nataliebuskethomas.com

RESEARCH CREDITS

http://www.dailymail.co.uk/sciencetech
http://www.ucsusa.org/food_and_agriculture
Wikipedia.com

PROLOGUE

President Ann Kinji waved her hand in front of the flat screen in front of her. Six hundred and seventy-nine Town Hall messages appeared. She prided herself on reading a sampling of these daily messages from American citizens every morning. After her fitness routine, and before breakfast, she skimmed through as many letters as she could in twenty minutes.

She pointed at the screen now to select the first message, eager to see what was waiting for her. It wasn't so much that she enjoyed these messages, although she did to some degree, but it was the time spent alone in her office that was so magical about her Town Hall sessions. Yes, Secret Service agents were just outside the door, and their presence was felt, in the same way that a dog made himself known when he was waiting outside the door for his people to come back, but nonetheless she was currently alone in the room, and she treasured every moment. She opened the first message.

<<Dear Madam President, Thank you for reversing the direction of the previous administration regarding government control of food, private farms, supplements, etc. I have a child who has food sensitivities and I need control over where our food comes from. As much as I'd like to grow all our own food, that's not realistic for me. The freedom to select natural foods that have not been restricted by government regulation is why I voted for you. I do have one issue though. You have taxed small farms and that higher cost is passed on to families like mine, but I'll take that. I do appreciate the lifting of regulations. >>

Ann smiled. The issue of food regulation had been the bane of her existence for several months of heated debate with Congress, farming representatives, and the Food and Health Administration, among others. It was good to see that her work was appreciated. So far so good, today's messages were positive. She opened another one.

<<Dear President Kinki, I spell your name Kinki because you is Kinki.>>

Ann laughed. Again? This was a message frequently seen in her inbox. There were always a few trolls in the mix, and this one seemed harmless, simply following the trend of sending variations on "Kinji is Kinki" that were sometimes humorous and creative, sometimes not. Most of the time these messages didn't make it past the spam filter, but every now and then one slipped through. She swiped her finger in the air to delete the message and move on to the next one.

<<President Kinji, you condemn past presidents because they rewrote the Constitution, and you are doing the same thing! Also, the idea of a Super Congress was brought up by debt ceiling negotiators back in 2011, and that is a change to the Constitution. I think you are a hypocrite. You did not have my vote, and WILL NOT have my vote! >>

Ann had heard similar rhetoric before, backlash over her recent remarks about the changes to the Constitution after the Big War. For every three Americans who wanted a reunited America, there was at least one American who wanted the union to stay divided. History had, on some level, repeated itself: even though the formerly-known-as-United States of America was split in two between East and West in a literal physical sense, it was the North and the South that were truly divided as a people. In general, the North wanted to reunite, while a growing number in the South wanted "less government", believing it was better to stay separate.

Ann shook off her fears about a civil war, should she be successful in reuniting America. With all the strategists and Generals working on possible scenarios, and all the technology in their vault, surely a civil war could be averted, or at the very least nipped in the bud quickly. She moved on from the critical e-mail and her brooding thoughts about potential civil unrest by opening the next message:

<<President Kinji, When my dog Macie was lost, I got her back because of the pet locator chip. I think all people should have these chips. You said you'd never even look at a bill to put identity chips on everyone at the DMV, to make everyone get a

chip when getting a driver's license. Why not? It's a good idea. If everyone got the chip I could find my ex-boyfriend. He unfriended me and I can't find him. If you cared about the American people you would care about this. Sincerely, Belinda>>

Ann chuckled, and then felt a twinge of guilt. This letter had a genuine feel to it. She selected "reply" and ignored the Identity Chip argument, which wasn't Belinda's real issue.

<<Dear Belinda, I'm sorry for the loss of your boyfriend. I know there is someone new in your future. Take good care of yourself, stay busy, volunteer to help others. You'll meet the right man when you are not looking.

Sincerely, President Kinji>>

Ann glanced at the clock. She had enough time to read a few more messages. She skimmed through a collection of similar letters: cranks, critics, fans, and the occasional off-topic, but sometimes extremely articulate, political rant. She kept going until she heard an alert: a new message had been sent from a code red mailbox – President's eyes only.

Ann stared at the screen impatiently, even though she was kept waiting for only two seconds.

There it was; a code red. She opened the message.

<<President Kinji, this is Penny. You might remember me? I was the driver for you and President Williams, one of the team of drivers, the one who was going to law school. I have something to tell you that I can't say in front of any of your secret service. Can you set me up with someone you trust outside of Chicago, someone who is totally unknown, with no agents? I'll meet that person in some way without agents or anyone listening. I don't know if you can do that, but I can't talk to you. They will know and they will kill me. I will send my friend to meet with whoever you want. I can't be seen with you, or anyone connected to you. Please, Madam President, there's not much time. They are watching me.>>

<<Penny, thank you for your bravery. Whatever you have to say, say it now, this is a secure line.>>

<<Not as secure as you think. They are tracking keywords. If I type anything with those keywords, they will see my message to you. Please, set me up with someone to talk to, in person. I have only a few minutes before they know I am gone. Please give me a name.>>

<<Serena Wilcox. You remember her? You'll have to travel. She's gone to Germany, of all places.>>

<<I will send my friend to her. And then Serena can meet with you.>>

There was a shrill beep: line closed.

Ann shook her head. What could this possibly be about? She sat and stewed about it for a few minutes, and then went to one committee meeting after another. At the end of a very long day, she picked up the phone to call Serena and give her a head's up.

Serena answered on the first ring.

"Serena? I know you're having a grand time abroad, and I hate to interrupt, but a friend of mine will be meeting with you soon to give you a message for me."

"Your friend has already found me, he's standing right here." Serena's voice sounded stilted. "But he's no friend, not unless you want me dead." And with that, the call was disconnected.

1

President Kinji tucked her hair behind her ears, a fruitless gesture since her signature bob was cut too short for hair to stay tucked over her ear lobes. She picked up a pencil and began chewing on the eraser, something she hadn't done since she was a child. Completely unaware of what she was doing, or the stunned looks on her staff's faces, she gnawed at the eraser until there was nothing left of it. Then she tossed the pencil back on the desk and formulated her thoughts. Finally, she spoke.

"So who's getting Serena out of there?" she

asked. It was unclear who she was addressing, so no one answered. Ann made eye contact with each of the five young people in the room. "Get me someone."

No one moved.

Ann said, "Get me my husband."

Everyone moved.

Ann surveyed the now-empty Oval Office. Could it be called Oval? The room had been built like a giant ice cube. She hated it. Hated, hated, hated it. She hated everything inside the walls of the closed society known as the new White House: the walls of ivory, beige, cream, tan, sand, caramel and "linen"; the soaring modern-day-architectural cathedral ceilings that created a chill not unlike the dreary drafts felt by monks in centuries-old monasteries, but without the ethereal air; the gaudy display of wealth represented by insanely priced presidential pens and an office chair with hand-sewn upholstery worth $10,000; and most of all, the plastic people holding her sequestered in this prison.

What kept her sane were the regular coffee chats with her dear friend Serena Wilcox, someone who didn't have a political bone in her body. Half the time, she didn't even watch the news. She was outside of the fray, untainted by the dirty fingers of lobbyists and power-hungry star-climbers. She was a pure outsider to "The Cube". Best of all, she was delightfully funny, unconventional, witty, and genuine. Ann had pushed hard for the friendship with Serena, as if Serena were a pet she adopted; needy and odd behavior coming from Ann, not Presidential in the slightest.

And now Ann had potentially killed her new pet. Too much affection can do that.

"It's not your fault," said Ted.

Ann moved away from her desk, where she had been glowering at a stack of ridiculously overpriced notepads. She had requested notepads due to her love-hate relationship with computerized planners and her lack of trust in any staffer to record her thoughts for her. Nonetheless, she despised the notepads. She could be using scratch paper like her Mom used to keep in the kitchen drawer by the phone – no need for her scribbles to take on such formality. Waste. No wonder the country was in such a mess.

"You have to know that you had nothing to do with this," Ted tried again.

"You and I both know that if she was not a personal friend of the President, she wouldn't be in this situation."

Ted shrugged with the resignation that all long-time-married men know, and said something wise that few men would realize to be the best answer for this situation and many others: "What do you want me to say?"

Ann mirrored Ted's shrugging and said, "I don't know. But while we stand here talking, Serena could be dead."

"We know the threat is credible?" asked Ted.

"I spoke to her myself. It came from Serena's own lips. Yes, credible."

Ted whistled; a low steady tone he had rehearsed to perfection.

Ann cringed. His "whistle of drama" got under her skin. She cracked every knuckle on both of her hands. Then Ted promptly did the same. We've been married too long, she thought. She smiled.

"What? You have an idea?"

"No," said Ann, "Just thinking that I'm glad you are here."

"Me too. Is her husband with her?"

"I don't know. Tom and the kids were with

11

her, but he was there for business. He could have been at work. The kids were probably with her though. I don't know anything, just guessing."

"What business does he have in Germany?"

"He works civil service now. He's there as support to a Guard unit that's over there on a routine two-week annual deployment."

"We're still doing that? Even with the bases over there closed?"

"Not all are closed. And yes, we are still doing that. Serena went with him to vacation, to show the kids all the famous hot spots in Europe."

"Any reason to suspect this is about what Tom is doing?"

"No, this is all me. Remember my driver Penny?"

"The one who wants to be a lawyer?"

"Yes. She sent me an e-mail right before this happened. She wanted to talk to someone I could trust, someone outside of The Cube."

"And you told her to talk to Serena?"

"Yes."

"Ah, I see."

"What is taking them so long?" Ann glanced at the mammoth screen on the wall: no new activity.

She stared at it for a few seconds, willing it with her mind to change. And it did. She and Ted raced to the center of the sensor range. Ted gestured for the menu to appear.

They read the simple message from Agent Donnelly: <<Bluebird flown. Nothing there.>>

Ann raised two fingers in the air to signal the teleconferencing function. She raised her voice even though it was sufficient to speak in normal conversational tones; she just couldn't quite get used to not having a phone at her ear while speaking over a connection. "Agent Donnelly, you there?"

"Yes, Madam President."

"She's gone then? What about her husband? The kids?"

"He is with us now, and the kids."

"Where were they? They weren't with Serena?"

"They were at the library."

"On the base?"

"Yes."

"So Serena was alone then? They got her at home?"

"Yes and yes. No trace. Sorry, Madam

President."

"Nothing at all?"

"They are sweeping the apartment now, but they aren't optimistic."

"I understand." Ann looked at Ted's face for any sign that he had an idea of what to do next. He didn't. After a long pause she resumed conversation. "Stay with Tom and the kids. Let me know if anything happens."

"Yes, Madam President."

"And Agent Donnelly?"

"Yes?"

"This is covert – me, you, Ted, and your team. That's it. Got it?"

"Yes, Madam President."

"Donnelly, your team is need-to-know."

"Understood."

"Follow protocol, but report to no one but me for now."

"We have a name for this operation?"

"Call it Covert Coffee."

2

Serena Wilcox Bridges, known professionally as Serena Wilcox, toyed with the idea of eating another slice of loaded and greasy pizza. "I don't eat pizza very often anymore."

"We could send Jeff out to get you something else. Taco? Burger?"

"No, it's okay, but no pizza again for me for a while." She had to admit it was fun to have American fast food again, but she would miss her favorite Gasthaus dishes, like Rahmschnitzel; veal served with a mushroom sauce made by sautéing

15

garlic and onions, adding red wine and heavy cream (Rahm), and allowing the sauce to thicken. Yet she felt her stomach complaining at the very thought of more rich foods. No, Rahmschnitzel would not be good after the jet lag, pizza, and kidnapping trifecta.

Serena surveyed the hotel room. It was pleasant enough, with its bland art in tasteful frames, its neutral walls, and strong smell of cleaning chemicals, but she knew if she had a black light she would see the proof of thousands of revolting human secrets.

"When do you think my husband and kids will be told I'm okay? When can I talk to them?"

"I don't know."

"I want to help President Kinji in any way that I can, and I stand by that decision, but Penny told me that my family wouldn't be left worrying about me. I'm not willing to put them through that."

"Sorry, I don't know. I'm just the bodyguard, and the butler I guess," said Agent Estep as he cleared Serena's plate away from the mahogany desk she had taken up residence in front of, having found a bit of personal space from the three men who sat in the small lounging area that contained a couch, a chair, an end table with a lamp on it, and two floor lamps.

All of the lamps were turned on, but even though the window blinds were closed, the powerful street lights in the parking lot outside the window illuminated the room, rendering the need for three lamps unnecessary. She appreciated the extra lighting – all the easier to see who she was dealing with.

Estep was a man in his early twenties; tall, dark and handsome; good looking enough to look like an actor, but humble enough to be refreshingly likeable. The only son in a family with five girls, Estep knew, respected, and enjoyed women, while also solidly bearing all of his father's testosterone-grounded hopes for the future fully and happily on his broad shoulders.

A man who was sensitive, funny, smart, and masculine who was still single? Not for long, thought Serena. "Can you get me in touch with Penny please?"

Serena caught Estep sizing her up, and he apparently deemed her to be trustworthy. "Yeah, I can do that." He pressed a couple of numbers and gave Serena his phone.

"Penny? This is Serena. Yes, I'm fine. One

thing though, you said that Tom and the kids wouldn't be left worried sick, wondering what happened to me. Yes, I understand, but that was my one condition when I agreed to do this. Yes, I can see that. Alright, if that's the best you can do. Thank you, Penny."

Estep took his phone back and raised his eyebrows. "Well?"

"She says they'll have to snatch Tom and the kids. It's the only way to protect them, and the only way to give them a message about me. She said it would have been easier if we'd been together when you took me, but now they'll have to do this separately."

"I see."

"They won't be brought here. Too risky that someone might follow them here. Best to bring them somewhere else."

"Those guys are good. Your family will be okay, don't worry."

"Thanks Estep."

"I doubt you'll be apart for long."

"I hope not. When can I get to work?"

"I can brief you now if you are ready."

"Yes, now is good." Serena's voice revealed

her surprise.

"I know, briefings are usually not delivered by the butler, but I'm a little higher up on the chain than I've led you to believe." Estep winked at her, a move that would have made a younger woman blush. Serena simply felt old and tired.

What am I caught up in? I should be home with my family, she thought. She wondered if anyone had checked on the dog to see if he needed fresh water. They hadn't gotten him an ISO pet microchip, jumped through hoops for a USDA certified veterinary form to obtain a pet passport, and flown him all the way to Germany only to have him die of dehydration! Aloud she said, "Please fill me in."

Estep folded his long lanky frame into the only available chair and pulled data up on his phone. "Look at this face. Ring any bells?"

Serena glanced at the photo. "Is it supposed to?"

"No, didn't think you'd know him."

"Who is he?"

"He is the man behind a lobbyist group. He's not happy about new legislation on the table." Estep pulled out a slim silver stylus and selected another photo from the database. He placed the phone into her hand. "Do you know this face?"

Serena glanced at the photo, did a double-take, and studied the photo more closely. "I think I do. He's older now than when I last saw him, but I think this is the same boy. I met him in Minnesota. He was a child prodigy, a computer genius, nice kid. What does he have to do with this?" Serena's curiosity was now piqued enough that her fatigue was forgotten.

"Nothing, but we've been following him, and grooming him for a scenario like this. He can help you find the people involved, track them via satellite and the typical footprints, and hook you up with any other technology you might need."

"I understand. But I still have no idea why I'm pretending to be kidnapped. Why did I tell Ann – President Kinji – that someone would kill me? I thought you said that she specifically asked for my help, so why doesn't she know what's going on? And, by the way, I don't know what's going on either."

"The President was warned by one of her staff that security has been compromised." Estep stopped talking and stared at her face for a long moment.

"Someone from the inside is involved."

"Yes, I understand what compromised means."

"That's why she asked for you."

"But why the kidnapping if she asked for me?"

"To protect the president. We know she trusts you, and we respect her judgment. So we got you. And it's in her best interest if she doesn't know what you are doing on her behalf."

"But aren't you drawing more attention to what we are doing? How is this helpful?" Serena raised her voice to be heard over the vacuuming din coming from the housekeeping service in the room next door.

Estep, with his deep baritone, did not need to raise his voice, but he did anyway. "Because the President has no idea that you are already working with us, she is protected from whatever happens."

"She's going to want to find me. I don't see how this is helpful. Am I not getting something?"

"She has assigned our team to an operation to recover you, and that is all she knows. We'll keep her briefed enough to occupy her, and anything you are doing meanwhile won't touch her."

"You do realize that I'm not an insider to anything, right? I solve mysteries, mainly over the computer. That's all I can offer. I still don't get all of this secrecy and drama."

"It's better that she think we're looking for you than for her to be briefed on what you are doing, which is what she would be ordering us to do if she knew you were working on this. If her office is compromised, and we are working on that assumption, we need to protect the President from even herself. We vetted you out, and you held up, but we can't do that with all certainty for everyone else that the President might think she can trust. So, if she doesn't know anything, she can't talk about it." This was the most Estep had said at one time, and he said it without seeming to breathe.

"I see. Smart plan. Did you come up with it?" Serena's antennae were raised. Who had the authority to make decisions in the name of security that went over Ann's head and without her knowledge?

"No it wasn't me. I don't go that far up the ladder, only a few rungs up from butler." Estep grinned, enjoying his butler joke beyond its expiration date. Seeing no reaction from Serena, he quickly switched gears, erasing his smirk and resuming the blank-faced expression of a solid

Secret Service Agent. "I can't tell you who is in charge, you'll have to trust the process. I already spent way more time explaining why you are here than I expected to. From now on, ask fewer questions. Once we get you set up, you'll have to work fast. We can't stall her for more than a couple of days."

"What happens if I can't figure this out before then?"

"Operation Covert Coffee will need a resolution. We'll tell her we've found you, and go from there."

"Operation Covert Coffee? That's what she's calling my rescue?"

"Yes."

"I like it." Serena smiled, basking in the glow of having an operation dedicated to her. "How did all of this start? Don't leave anything out."

Estep's only response was to scowl at Serena. His handsome face was instantly transformed into that of an intimidating, flint-eyed thug – a side of him that his sisters and mother had never seen. He unfolded himself from the chair he had occupied for only a few minutes. "We have to move you."

"Already?" Serena looked around the room,

startled at the sudden turn of events. "You don't think we are safe enough here?"

"My alert sounded." Estep pointed to his ear, where a microchip was hidden, communicating with him at all times.

Serena grabbed her purse and hurried out the door. Estep was quickly met by a team of equally athletic and capable agents that swallowed the petite detective so completely that she was invisible from outside of the swarm. It was with this entourage that she walked from one room to another, shuffling along at a steady but manic pace.

Once inside the room, Estep took up position in an identical chair to the one he'd been in just moments earlier. "We are secure now. Let's proceed."

"What? We only moved up a floor. How is that more secure?"

"We won't be staying in the same place for more than thirty minutes at a time. Keeping you moving is a precaution."

"How can I get anything done if I'm moving around all the time?"

"Only until we get you to the computer lab. You'll stay there as long as it takes."

"Is that why you brought me back to Minnesota? Are we talking about the same lab where I saw the boy in the photo? I remember his name is Nicholas."

"Yes, same lab. Nicholas will be there when you arrive."

"I didn't realize the lab was still in use. I guess I assumed it would be shut down."

"No, it was claimed by the agency."

"Which agency?"

Estep raised his eyebrows.

"Asking too many questions?"

Estep growled.

"I'd like to talk to my family. When would that be possible?"

Estep stared back at her, his face void of all expression. Several seconds passed. Serena studied the framed art on the wall – same bland factory prints as in the previous room, same color scheme, slightly different subject matter. The paintings struck her as funny for no real reason, and she looked away before she started laughing. She was feeling the weight of the jet lag, and fatigue from everything else too. She wondered when the agents would leave her alone so that she could sleep, if she could sleep.

"I'm here of my own free will, I don't see why I should be denied talking to my family and making sure that they are okay."

Estep's expression remained unchanged. His eyes didn't even seem to blink.

"I am here of my own free will, right?"

"Define 'free will'", said Estep.

3

Lora put her purse on the belt and allowed herself to be patted down. She didn't mind the "wanding" but the frisking got a little out of hand. She leered at the guard. "Enjoying yourself?"

The guard ignored her.

Oh, so that's it, then, I'm not good enough to talk to? Lora bristled. She knew his type. He probably had a plain wife sitting at home, chasing after his freckle-faced sticky-fingered rug-rats, cooking his dinners, and watching the clock for when he would be home. Well, Lora would never be that wife: she was good enough to touch, but not good enough to marry. Story of her life. She scooped her purse off the conveyor belt, opened it as she walked away from the security check-in, dug for her signature vial of Tic Tacs, flipped open the plastic lid, popped one in her mouth, and returned the Tic Tacs to her purse, all without missing a step.

"You can't go in there," said a female Special Agent named Carla Keefer. Keefer's red hair bobbed upon her shoulders in coils of thick curls while unruly tendrils framed her face. So sweet and lovely was she that it was difficult for her to be taken seriously as an agent.

Lora scoffed at her now. "I'm just going to sit down." She darted for the row of chairs situated behind the ropes. Keefer snatched her by the arm and yanked her elbow behind her back, dragging her back within the confines of the holding area.

"Hey! You didn't have to do that!" Lora yelped.

"Stay behind the ropes," Keefer said simply. She locked eyes with Lora, but did not engage her. Her stare-down was firm, no-nonsense, and dismissive; a combination that asserted her authority over Lora in an instant. Of course the show of force had already paved the way for that.

Lora gave her no more trouble; she waited in compliance, standing, shifting her weight from one foot to the other, sighing every few seconds.

"Come with me," said Keefer. She led Lora down a long tiled corridor. Lora's high-heeled pleather fashion boots clicked with every step, announcing her arrival long before her slender frame reached the conference room. Keefer opened the door for her, gestured for her to go in, nodded to the agents inside, and left, leaving Lora behind. More than one agent stared out the windowed door at Keefer's curvy figure as she turned away. Lora rolled her eyes. Men are all the same, she thought.

"Sit down," said Agent Browning.

Lora slid her long manicured fingers along the top of the back of the only chair at the table. When her fingers reached the end, she eased her body into the seat of the chair, imagining her movements to be slinky and sexy. She then studied her fingers, admiring the fingernail art on each painted nail.

The agents were unimpressed. Browning pulled a second chair up to the table, directly across from where Lora was perched. "Do you know why you are here?" he began.

"The President wants to have me to dinner?"

"Is that your final answer?"

"This is about my e-mail? It was a joke."

"Before sending the message you consented to the contract between yourself and this office. When you added your virtual signature, your consent to our terms was recorded and verified."

"I didn't read it."

"Your signature indicates that you have waived your right to object to any inquiry we may make into the source, content, or intent behind your message."

"I didn't sign anything."

"You selected the option allowing this office to assign a virtual signature to your message. It was required before the message was allowed to be sent. Whether you remember doing it or not, we have records of you having done so. Would you like to see our records?"

"No," said Lora dejectedly.

"Do you understand that the purpose of this inquiry is to establish the intention behind your message? Do you also understand that you are here of your own accord and can leave at any time?"

"I guess so."

"Please describe your message and explain why you sent that message to the Town Hall forum, to President Ann Kinji, recipient."

"It was a joke – Kinji is Kinki – everyone does it. It's yesterday by now, not even funny anymore. Thought it was funny when I wrote it. Do I look like a terrorist?"

"Why did you write it?"

"I told you, it was a joke."

"What made you decide to send it?"

"Someone dared me. I can't remember who. It was at a bar. I sent it from my phone."

"Who told you to do it?"

"I said, I don't remember who."

"Does that happen often, that you don't remember who you are talking to?"

Lora threw her head back to give her hair a good toss. "What do you think? They know my name there."

"Are you saying you were intoxicated when you sent the message to the President?"

Lora snorted. "Yes! I'm saying I was wasted. Can I go now?"

"Yes, you can go now. Agent Keefer will escort you out. But Ma'am?"

"Ma'am!"

"Miss?"

"Better."

"No more drunk-dialing the President."

On that note, Lora left the heart of American government behind her as she clicked and clacked her way down the long corridors and back out into the outside world, where a cab was waiting for her. She got in without saying anything to the driver, ignored the seat belt, and flipped open her phone.

"Vic? Yeah, it's me. Yeah, I did it. No, they didn't see me. I attached it to the table, underside like you said. No, they didn't notice, too busy staring at my chest. Nobody's listening, Victor. Okay, okay, see you soon."

Lora looked down at her fingers. The nail art on her left ring finger was down to one layer, like all of her other fingernails. However, before she entered the interrogation room, that nail had had two layers. One was nail art, like now. The top layer had been a tiny film, containing a microchip, which was now recording everything said in the interrogation room.

Why Victor wanted her to do this, she didn't know. But he was paying her good money and that was all she cared about. He had paid her at the bar to send the message, and he had promised her more money today, at the hotel room where she was going.

What Lora was about to find out was that Victor had no intention of seeing Lora again, and when his people were done with her, no one else would ever see her again either. So it is unfortunate then that Lora didn't enjoy the view from her cab passenger window, because it was the last time she would ever see the great city that she loved, or anything else for that matter.

4

Serena was back in Minnesota and boy could she feel it! The air was so dense with cold that her lungs hurt when she breathed. Brisk, baby! Brr! She rubbed her hands together and felt herself grinning from ear to ear.

"This is freaking August," Agent Estep complained. He bent his head against the wind that was ripping across the tarmac on a private runway near the International airport in Minneapolis-Saint Paul.

Beyond the tarmac, early morning light was

barely coming up over the low horizon, a horizon foreign to those who had never seen a Northern skyline before. Serena described the Minnesotan sky as a low ceiling, like the skyline of a snow globe when tilted at an angle. The sky-ceiling felt claustrophobic to her, especially when compared to the higher clouds found nearly everywhere else in the nation. Chicken Little would have really thought that the sky was falling if he lived here, she thought.

And yet, instead of feeling the old dread about Earth-hugging clouds, dense air, and Canadian chill, she felt nearly giddy to be back on Minnesotan soil. While Serena had lived in many places throughout her forty-plus years, she had spent most of her adult life in the Twin Cities area and she now thought of it as home. Home. So good to be back.

"Where is the lab? We aren't headed back to the Cannon Falls area," said Serena.

"No, it's been moved."

"To?"

"Wisconsin."

"Wisconsin!"

"Not far, thirty miles from here. Near Hudson. It's an old Girl Scout camp, no longer used for scouting, obviously."

"Obviously."

"The original building that housed the campers is still on site. You'll be staying there."

"I'm familiar with Hudson. I've been to the lakefront there with my family. Got some gyros, and sunburn because we forgot sunscreen. We went downtown later, very cute. It was all lit up and I couldn't believe how populated it was, really hopping. We wanted to go to that Pier 51 restaurant, could smell the food and saw the outdoor dining was packed, but we didn't make it there."

Estep didn't reply.

Serena gave up on conversation, and in the silence that followed, could hear a faint voice, a narration-sounding voice. She strained her eyes a little to study his ears. Ah, plugged in! It appeared Estep was listening to an audio book. Serena tried not to take it personally. If she were a young guy in his 20s, she wouldn't find herself interesting either.

The rest of the trip passed by quickly. Serena was so tired that the silence was welcome. She allowed her thoughts to drift. What am I in for, and will I really be of any use to President Kinji? Will I even know what to do? And when will I see my family again?

She hadn't felt homesick in a long time, because ever since she'd become a mother, she was seldom alone, even if away from home. She had forgotten how miserable homesickness was. Whether one is a child at camp, a student at college, a soldier at war, or was a middle-aged mother-of-three sequestered off to a secret government computer lab, the heart felt the same – heavy, dark, empty. She wanted to cry, but she held herself together. Again, she questioned why she was the President's best option, a question Estep had been pondering from the first mention of Serena's involvement in Covert Coffee.

"Here we are," said Estep. Serena noticed that he had recaptured his good humor, probably from having had a break from entertaining her in the quiet car. He had also received a text from his girlfriend, a fact that Serena had correctly assumed based on the goofy grin plastered on Estep's face when he thought Serena wasn't looking. This in-a-new-relationship repartee renewed the spring in his step, for which Serena felt his girlfriend deserved a medal. "You should find everything you need here."

"I still don't know what it is that I'll be doing."

"You'll figure it out. Go on in." Estep unlocked three sections of a nearly invisible door via a pre-programmed code on his phone. The door slid open and closed immediately after sensing the two had entered. It snapped shut so quickly that Serena made a mental note never to reach back suddenly after passing through the entry – she could lose an arm!

"Hi, Mrs. Meadows," said Nicholas cheerfully.

"Meadows? Haven't heard that name in a long time," Serena said, looking as if she had tasted something sour. "It was an alias, Nicholas. I'm Serena Wilcox Bridges. You can call me Serena."

"Miss Serena?"

"Sure." Serena smiled. She liked polite children. He had won her over already. This would be an easy assignment, except for the obvious fact that she had no idea what they were doing.

"You can use that computer over there," said Nicholas. He pointed at the sleek blue model on his left.

"Wow, this lab is fantastic! How did you get this setup?" Serena gushed.

The lab was futuristic, and vibrant. The color

scheme looked familiar, but she couldn't quite place it. Nicholas' next comment answered her unspoken question.

"I am a Superman fan."

Serena laughed. "That would explain the blue, red, and yellow machines." She glanced at the walls. "And the posters of course."

Nicholas pointed at the ceiling.

Serena laughed again. "Ah! And there's the man of steel himself!" A large mural of Superman, with fisted arm outstretched, red cape unfurled behind him, in classic flight pose, had been artfully painted on the domed ceiling.

"Goodness, they must think a lot of you, Nicholas."

Nicholas smiled modestly and nodded.

"Makes me wonder what it is that you do for them to get such royal treatment."

Nicholas didn't answer.

Estep came out of nowhere and clapped a gloved hand on Serena's shoulder. "No more questions."

Startled, Serena spun around to look Estep in the face. If she'd had any experience with bears clapping her on the shoulder, she would have described it as similar to being clapped on the shoulder by Agent Estep, minus the claws – those were only implied. "I wasn't seriously trying to press him for answers."

Estep didn't step back. Instead, he drew himself in closer and stayed inside Serena's personal space for the duration of the conversation. "His role here is not your business. Stay on task."

"I don't even know what my task is," Serena tried again, in vain, to get some direction.

"My shift with you is over," said Estep, without disappointment. "Behave yourself, or they'll call me back."

"And you wouldn't like to come back?" Serena smiled sweetly.

"You wouldn't like it if I have to come back." And on that note Estep left the lab without so much as a wave.

"He's crabby today," said Nicholas.

"I ask too many questions," said Serena simply.

Nicholas shrugged. "You better stop that then." He jerked his head toward the back of the room where the next agent-in-charge was already in place.

Serena slid her chair closer to Nicholas and whispered, "They aren't keeping you here against your will are they?"

Nicholas shook his head no.

Serena tried again, "Do you need any help?"

Nicholas turned his chair to look her in the eyes. "I like it here. There is nothing wrong. We should get to work."

Serena studied his face and saw that he was telling her the truth. "Okay then, tell me what to do."

Nicholas' long reach allowed him to tap Serena's monitor without leaving his chair. "Read these."

Serena blinked at the screen. She thought she knew what she was looking at, but she wasn't sure. "Is this what I think it is? Is this President Kinji's private e-mail account?"

"Kind of. It's the Town Hall e-mail."

"This is a more comprehensive list than the few samples published for the general public to see."

"Yeah, this is all of them."

"For? The week?"

"No, just one day."

"And I'm looking for?"

Nicholas shrugged. "I don't know. I just give you the data."

"And she doesn't know you have this?" Serena felt like she was catching on now. This really was work that she could do with her private investigator experience, and the best part was that she didn't have to collect the intelligence herself.

"When you are done with that, listen to this." Nicholas removed his dapper wool cap, an unusual accessory for a boy his age. He peeled a sliver of material off the underside brim of the cap and handed it to Serena.

"What is this? It looks like a fingernail."

"It is a fingernail."

"What?" Serena blanched. She could take blood, she could take gore, but she hated gross human stuff like hair, mucus, and fingernails.

"The nail is a bug."

"How do I play it?"

"Insert it under the audio scanner," said Nicholas, standing up and moving toward her machine. "Like this."

"I see. And it will upload to the computer?"

"Yep. And the audio file can play directly off

the scanner too. You can use those ear buds." He gestured toward the plastic packet containing tiny Superman-colored wireless ear buds. They were so small that Serena feared she would lose them before she could attach them to her ears.

"Where is the bug from? Not President Kinji's office without her consent, I hope?"

"No. It's from the interrogation room, interviewing the Town Hall people."

"The ones who wrote those e-mails?"

"Yes."

"So they think that the person, or persons, we are looking for wrote one of those e-mails?"

"They don't think, they know."

"How do they know?"

"The lady who put that bug in the room is dead."

5

Agent Estep was back on Chicago soil. The sprawling city was home to the newly re-united States of America, as the D.C. area was still in recovery post Big War. The White House had been built quickly, with most of the rooms still unfinished, unfurnished, and uninspired. It seemed that no one embraced the idea of a White House in Chicago, and Estep suspected that the building would never be finished. As soon as D.C. was deemed inhabitable again, he was certain that they'd all be headed back home. But meanwhile, here he was, outside of the building where President Ann Kinji was serving a second term as President of the United States of a recently divided America, a war-torn and politics-shy nation. And while they continued to slug their way forward, it was obvious from present events that there were some who didn't want to let go of the past.

Estep wondered who those people were, and if he would ever find them. His role in Covert Coffee was to head the team protecting Serena Wilcox, a task he felt was beneath his pay grade. He consoled himself with the fact that he wasn't restricted from following leads that would indirectly protect Ms. Wilcox; at least that was what he told the two junior agents he brought with him to Victor's door.

Victor didn't respond to the doorbell or the vigorous rapping on the door.

"Do we go in?" asked Agent Champlin.

"No warrant," said Agent Bonifield.

Estep pulled out a sophisticated set of lock picks. He opened the door in seconds. He drew his gun, entered the apartment, and immediately found Victor, alive and well, sitting on the couch watching TV.

Estep did not lower his gun. "Why didn't you

answer the phone or the door, you hiding from us, Victor?"

"Not from you, from them."

"Who?"

Victor shut off the TV. "The ones who killed Lora. They'll be after me next."

"And why would they do that? We know you're the one who hired them to kill her." Estep was in all-out interrogation mode, using every ounce of his bulky physical presence to intimidate the defeated looking man on the couch. He had the deep voice of condemnation, the furrowed brow of the accuser, and the arms of an enforcer. But none of these were necessary.

Victor began to sob. At first it was a confusing sound, a mix between a snort and a hiccup. The agents exchanged glances, thinking that he might be getting sick. Then the sobbing grew louder, and it was clear that the man was crying with full abandon. The three men subconsciously backed away from the couch, and tried not to look directly at the man's face.

Agent Bonifield left the room in search of a tissue box. He returned with a new box of tissues. Estep grabbed the box out of his hands, ripped off the perforated top, tossed the cardboard packaging on the floor, and threw the box at Victor, who did not catch it. Victor picked the box up and spent the next few minutes alternating between blowing his nose and crying.

Estep dragged a chair closer to the couch and sat in it. "Enough already! Start talking."

"They'll kill me."

"So will we."

Victor froze in mid-blow, his tissue at his nose. His eyes were as wide open as a clown's; his face just as pale, his nose just as red. With Victor's bald head and tufts of red hair on the sides, he could join a circus.

The junior agents nearly suffered from whiplash after whirling around to gawk at Estep. One of them dared speak up. "I won't be a part of this," he croaked, his voice barely above a whisper.

"Then go," said Estep. "Now!"

Agent Champlin fled out the door. Agent Bonifield stayed rooted in his place, but his facial expression revealed his desire for the floor to open up and swallow him whole.

"You too. Get!" Estep snarled.

Victor shrank into the couch, cowering and

clutching his saturated tissue. "I'll tell you what I know," he said in a trembling falsetto.

Estep sighed. The ease of this interrogational breakdown was absurd; his agents and this sniveling idiot were cowards. Some days, the agency didn't pay him enough. He drew his chair even closer to Victor. He growled, "No, we'll start with what I know."

Victor gave up his slouch and cower routine, reassured that he was not facing imminent death. He peered into Estep's eyes to gauge the level of the threat. Estep was pleased to note that Victor saw nothing but unwavering canine focus on the target. Victor resumed his slouch. "I'm listening," he said.

"We contracted you to create the bug and outfit Lora with it. We vetted you before the hire. There was nothing in your background to suggest that you were anything but a patriot and upstanding citizen. So what happened, Victor? Did you lose money at the races? You aren't the traitor we were looking for, but you know who he is. He found you before we found him."

Victor blinked rapidly, saying nothing.

"Who bought you?" Estep hissed, his question more of a strangled exclamation.

Victor sat up straight, the flicker of recognition in his eyes. "Oh, that's what you think! No, no, you've got it all wrong. I'm the victim here – isn't that obvious? I don't have the stones to be a double agent; your words, not mine. I barely had the courage to work for the good guys. You can search the apartment. I have no weapons. I don't even have a dog. You saw for yourself how easy it was to walk right in and threaten me."

Estep nodded. "Agreed. So that's your story then? You were threatened?"

Victor began gesturing with his arms in big loopy circles, looking so much like Bozo that Estep had to suppress the urge to grin. "Yes, I was threatened! They wanted me to tell them everything, or else they would kill me, but not without torturing me first. They showed me they meant business too!"

"How so? Did they hurt you?"

"No, but they did take Henry."

"Your son?"

"No, I don't have any kids."

"Who's Henry?"

"My computer. I give all my computers names. Henry holds a lot of data, data that is encrypted and only someone of my caliber could hack it, but nonetheless, they stole my work."

"What are you mixed up in, Victor?"

"Oh no, it's nothing like that. Again, you jumped to the wrong conclusion. This information is research type stuff, statistics."

"So you sold out your country, and got Lora killed, over nothing – over the theft of your computer?"

"Lora's dead?" Victor gasped. His mouth formed a large O, his face a mask of horror and terror.

"You are trying my patience. You better start making sense." Estep leaned in close to Victor's face and let his hot angry breath unfurl onto Victor's forehead. "Tell me what I want to know. Now!" He slammed his hand on the coffee table, causing everything on the table to bounce, clatter, or tip over. Water spilled and trickled off the edge of the table, making a steady dripping sound onto the well-worn pea-green shag carpet.

"Okay, okay! I'll try to say it more clearly. Three men came into the apartment, just like you three did today. They said that they knew I was working for the government and that they needed to know what it was that I was doing."

"And you told them?" Estep let his disgust show on his face.

"The one like you, the big one? He held a gun at my head. So, yes, I told them."

"And when you finished telling them, they left?"

"Not without taking Henry, and flushing my turtle down the toilet." Tears began to flow at the thought of his turtle being flushed. "They told me they'd be back for me if I didn't tell them everything I knew, and they'd hack me up, and flush me down the toilet along with Jared."

"The turtle?"

"Yes, Jared is my turtle. Poor Jared." Victor was sobbing now, and nearing the bottom of what had been a full box of tissues. His used tissues were wadded up and laid on the cushion next to him, and had created quite a pile.

"Who are these men?"

Victor pulled the tissue away from his face, surprised. "How should I know?"

"These men knew a lot about you. They knew about your computer, and they knew you'd be upset if they flushed your turtle. I, for example, wouldn't have gone for your turtle. I would have shot your knee cap." Estep drew out his gun and held it against Victor's bended knee.

"You don't have to do that! Put the gun away, put it away, put it away!" Victor shrieked the same words over and over until Estep removed the gun from his knee.

"So who are they?" Estep scowled in the menacing manner that he had rehearsed in front of the mirror. He nailed that look, and was pleased to see the effect it had on Victor. Even better than the gun, he thought with satisfaction.

"Okay, okay. Yes, I know them." Victor dropped his head in defeat; staring dramatically at the floor, letting his arms fall limply at his sides. "Are you going to arrest me now?"

Estep gritted his teeth. Oh how he wanted to hit this clown. "Just tell me who they are."

"They are security for FYD."

"FYD?"

"Food Yield and Development."

Now it was Estep's turn to be surprised. "The lobbyist group?"

"Yes."

"Do you have that information on any other

computer?"

Victor scoffed. "Of course I have back-up. I have back-up to the back-up. I always save my data in triplicate. At least. I know it's on Emily."

"Which one is Emily?"

Victor pointed to the iMac in the back of the room.

"Really? How can you encrypt on that thing? My dad used one of those when he was in college."

Victor rolled his eyes. "It's just a shell of an iMac, for kicks, vintage. The guts are state of the art technology, a dream system you wouldn't even know what to do with."

"Unplug it, get it ready. We're taking it with us."

"Us? By us you mean you and those two agents?"

"No, by us I mean me and you."

"Where are we going?"

"To Wisconsin.".

6

Serena could get used to working in the secret Superman computer lab. She had coffee, yogurt, and Chocolate Peanut Butter Bugles for breakfast; enjoyed a two-hour-long video chat with Tom and the kids after Nicholas got them connected (while Estep was away and unaware); and sank herself into a deep leather chair behind the luxury metallic-blue computer model of the future.

Serena laughed, a sound that Nicholas responded to by rotating his chair a few degrees via the wireless digital controls on his computer screen.

"Are these Town Hall messages always this nutty?" she asked.

"I don't know. I didn't read them," said Nicholas, disappointed that Serena's laugh wasn't a response from a joke, funny video, or anything else that might interest him. He rotated his chair back to its position in front of his own machine.

Serena was nearly finished reading through the hundreds of Town Hall messages. While President Kinji only received a cross section of messages, Serena had been given every message that had been submitted during the 24 hour period in question. Highlighted were the messages that Kinji had seen, and Serena suspected that those were the ones she should be focusing on. Because, whatever was going on, wouldn't the person or persons involved have found a way to get their message through? After all, they had become a serious threat of some kind. If their message, or messages, had hit the slush pile, never seen by Ann or her core people, would Serena be here right now? She thought not. She puzzled it out now, talking to herself. Nicholas glanced her way a few times, frowned, and looked away. Apparently Serena was throwing off his mojo.

"Nicholas? How do I use this bug reader scanner thing again?" Serena smiled sweetly. She rummaged in her purse for a pack of watermelon flavored gum that she had been saving for an emergency Tooth Fairy present for Rosie. She found the gum and kept it hidden inside her hand, her hand still in her purse.

Nicholas demonstrated the scanner again. As he turned back to his own work Serena tapped him on the shoulder and presented him with the pack of gum. Nicholas grinned. "Thanks!"

Yes, Serena could get used to working in this lab. Kids were so much easier to work with than adults. Just think; she could come to work with her purse loaded for bear: yo-yos, harmonicas, candy, and gag toys. Co-worker problems solved instantly. Nicholas was in a mellow mood now, smacking away at his new bubble gum. He had an entire pack of gum to himself; big smile, sunny attitude, problem solved.

Serena wished a pack of gum would work on Estep and grinned at the thought. She didn't smile for long though, what she heard on the fingernail bug was disturbing. She knew this voice to be Lora's – the woman who had planted the bug and was then promptly murdered.

Listening to Lora's voice nagged at Serena's conscience. Isn't this a violation of privacy, a disrespect of the dead? And yet, if I can help find her killer the end justifies the means.

Serena prepared herself for a heavy session of investigation by visualizing her ears hard-wired to her brain so that she could have total recall of the information later. But since that memory trick didn't always work, she also took notes via computer keyboard. She increased the volume, pulled the file back to the starting position, and listened to the recording from the beginning:

First was the sound of a chair scraping across the floor and then a male voice said, "Do you know why you are here?"

A female voice that Serena knew belonged to Lora said, full of sarcasm: "The President wants to have me to dinner?"

The male voice, sounding flat and unemotional, said: "Is that your final answer?"

Serena stopped the recording. "Nicholas, who is the agent questioning Lora?"

Nicholas swiped his screen a few times until he found the data file he was looking for. "I see

Agent Keefer listed, but she's a lady."

"Can you get me the name? If you can't, it might not be important anyway." Serena didn't want to send the kid on a wild goose chase.

"Give me a minute." Nicholas thumbed through the file for a few seconds. "Got it. His name is Gary William Browning."

"Agent Gary Browning?" Serena asked just to be clear.

"Yes."

"Thanks, Nicholas." Serena noted that Nicholas was already back to work on whatever it was that he was doing. She resumed the play-back of the recording:

Lora said: "This is about my e-mail? It was a joke." Serena picked up something in Lora's pitch. Lora was not at all surprised that she was being questioned about the e-mail. Which begged the question "Why not?" Had she sent the e-mail to catch the attention of the White House?

Browning said in a reading-straight-off-the-paper voice: "Before sending the message you consented to the contract between yourself and this office. When you added your virtual signature, your consent to our terms was recorded and verified."

"I didn't read it." Serena made note that Lora's flippant response didn't sound worried. The flippancy wasn't defensive; it was -- something else. Bored.

So, why was Lora so blasé about the whole thing? She was confident she wasn't going to be in any serious trouble. Why was she confident? Was she arrogant and ignorant, or did she know that someone powerful would protect her? Hmm. Serena clacked away at the keyword: Who did Lora know? What connections does she have?

Browning said, again revealing no insight into his emotional state; still sounding like he was reading from a script: "Your signature indicates that you have waived your right to object to any inquiry we may make into the source, content, or intent behind your message."

Lora said, with the same flippant tone, "I didn't sign anything."

Browning continued, "You selected the option allowing this office to assign a virtual signature to your message. It was required before the message was allowed to be sent. Whether you remember doing it or not, we have records of you having done so. Would you like to see our records?"

Serena typed: I want to see those records! Her fingernails hit the keyboard with such clatter that Nicholas turned his head to see what she was doing.

Since she already had Nicholas' attention, she said aloud, "I want to see Browning's records. I assume he means the e-mail trail, her IP address or smart phone trace, iPad, iPod, Implant Chip, or whatever else she was using."

"On it," said Nicholas cheerfully. Serena was back in his good graces now that she was giving him work to do, and of course the watermelon bubble gum didn't hurt either.

"Another thing, was anyone else present? Anyone who isn't on the audio file or in the log?"

Nicholas shook his head. "No, I don't think so, not unless you count the vice president."

"Morgan Canon was there? Yes, I count the VP. Why was he there?"

"I don't know, all I see is that the security detail reported that he checked in."

"Okay, good to know." Serena turned her focus back to the audio file.

Lora said no to Browning's offer to see her records. Serena noted that Lora sounded genuinely disinterested – not playing a game. Lora was either very simple, very confident, or both.

Browning continued, "Do you understand that the purpose of this inquiry is to establish the intention behind your message? Do you also understand that you are here of your own accord and can leave at any time?"

"I guess so." Again, Lora sounded bored, impatient to leave. She did not sound at all intimidated, anxious, or angry. Just restless. Distracted? Already thinking about where she was headed next?

Browning's tone remained unchanged. "Please describe your message, and explain why you sent that message to the Town Hall forum, to President Ann Kinji, recipient."

Lora perked up at this point, seemingly enjoying her response. "It was a joke – Kinji is Kinki – everyone does it. It's yesterday by now, not even funny anymore. Thought it was funny when I wrote it. Do I look like a terrorist?"

Browning said, revealing nothing, "Why did you write it?"

Lora stated, not defensively that Serena could tell, but simply stating the facts, "I told you, it was a joke."

Browning followed up with, "What made you decide to send it?" Serena couldn't get a read on Browning at all. He seemed like a guy doing his job, nothing personal that she could detect.

"Someone dared me. I can't remember who. It was at a bar. I sent it from my phone." This sounds rehearsed, scripted. Hmm. Serena made note of that in her file, both her mental file and her typed one.

Browning finally sounded like he was interested in hearing Lora's response. "Who told you to do it?"

"I said, I don't remember who."

Serena heard the sound of Browning writing something on a notepad. Filing out a report, doing his job. "Does that happen often, that you don't remember who you are talking to?"

Lora's voice reverted back to the sarcasm she'd displayed at the beginning of the interrogation. "What do you think? They know my name there."

Browning followed up, his voice flat again, losing interest. "Are you saying you were intoxicated when you sent the message to the President?"

Lora snorted. "Yes! I'm saying I was wasted.

Can I go now?" Serena's lie detector went off. Interesting. Why the storytelling?

Browning wrapped up, "Yes, you can go now. Agent Keefer will escort you out. But Ma'am?" After a pause, Browning said, louder, "Ma'am!" Another pause. Browning said, "Miss?"

Lora said, "Better."

Browning said, "No more drunk-dialing the President."

Serena didn't hear anything in Agent Browning's voice to make her doubt that he was doing his job, nothing more. She didn't think of Browning as a person of interest, not at all. In fact she made note not to bother looking into him. However, she did want to know what records he had, so she listened intently when Nicholas told her what he found.

"Agent Browning had Lora's e-mails, which I already sent you. He didn't have anything else. Well, except for her criminal record. She didn't do anything really bad, but this is weird."

"What did she do?" asked Serena.

"It says charge of public intoxication. That means drinking beer on the street, right?"

"Something like that, yes. What's weird?"

"She was arrested with that guy that Agent Estep is bringing in."

"Bringing in? What guy?"

As coincidence would have it, Agent Estep graced their presence at that very moment. He escorted an odd-looking clown-faced man into the building, a man who surveyed the lab with greedy anticipation.

Nicholas groaned. "Looks like he'll be working here too. That's the guy. Victor."

Estep stopped in his tracks. "Nick, what did you just say?"

"That's the guy. Serena asked me to look up Lora's background check. Victor was listed on her criminal record."

Estep leaped at Victor in a pounce like a cougar attacking his prey. Victor, slow on the take and not anticipating an ambush, gave up the fight immediately, letting his body go completely limp. Estep caught him before he fell on the floor, swept him up by his upper arms, and bent both arms behind the man's back. He cuffed them at the wrists and threw his body into the nearest chair, a chair that was, unfortunately for Victor, on wheels. This time Estep didn't catch him before he hit the floor.

Serena and Nicholas, both on their feet, peered down at the sprawled and cuffed form of a man on the floor.

Serena said, "Are you going to explain this?"

Estep said, "I was going to ask you the same thing."

7

Victor squirmed and rolled around on the floor slowly, like a slug in a salt shower. His bloated body even resembled a slug's. But it was his clown-like head that was the finishing touch to create a hideous blend of comedy and horror.

Estep looked like he was ready to spit on the man, Nicholas stared in fascination, and Serena averted her eyes, only to bring them back around to Victor again. She couldn't help herself. It was a train wreck situation.

"I didn't do anything, I didn't do anything!"

Victor squealed.

Estep grunted and snorted like a bull. Serena expected him to follow through on what looked like an intention to spit on Victor's hideous moon face, but he showed restraint. When Victor's squealing died down, Estep said, "We vetted you. And yet, you had a criminal record. Someone messed with your files to make you look clean. Who are you working for, Victor?"

"Help me up! I'm not saying anything until I'm off the floor and these cuffs are off," said Victor.

Estep grabbed him by the arm and yanked him up, causing Victor to wince. He shoved him into the nearest chair and said, "Cuffs stay on. Talk!"

Nicholas said, "Agent Estep, I can find out who changed his files. It will only take me a short time."

Estep nodded at the child genius, and said, "Thanks, buddy, you do that. But this maggot is going to tell me right now." He growled at Victor, bending close to him until his face was an inch from Victor's pale sweaty head.

Serena glanced at Nicholas. "Agent Estep, we should bring Victor into another room, don't you think?" She jerked her head toward the boy who had already turned toward the computer. Maybe Nicholas was desensitized to violence, but that didn't make the situation any more appropriate. Thankfully Estep agreed.

Since Victor's chair was on wheels, it was easy for the two of them to roll him into the office. Estep shut the door and pulled up a chair directly facing Victor, their knees touching. Serena remained standing, in a position deep into the corner of the office – just in case things started to get a little rough. And things did, immediately.

Serena had shielded Nicholas' young eyes from seeing the madness, but hearing what was going on in that room was unavoidable. Estep barked and growled like a pit bull, while Victor squealed like a stuck pig. The mingling of the two sounded like a farmyard brawl.

Serena contemplated leaving the room. How much longer would this play out? She counted ceiling tiles, shuffled her feet, and read every poster on the wall. Just when she felt she could take it no longer, the noise ceased. After a momentary pause in the action, in which both men wiped spittle off their lips, the exchange finally settled down into a real interrogation.

"Are you ready to tell me what you know?" asked Estep. He was calm now, controlled. Serena wondered if Estep's drama was all an act from start to finish or if the man really was unstable. Either he was very good or very much in need of an anger management course.

"What you told me before is that the FYD is behind this, and sent thugs to scare you," Estep began.

Serena asked, "FYD is the Food and what?"

"Food Yield and Development. Something the previous administration had in the works, but nothing went forward with it. After war and hell broke loose, FYD disappeared – yet still technically exists as a matter of record. Lobbyists are keeping FYD alive, barely. Not a big newsmaker, and not on anyone's radar. If you ask me, staying informed is the responsibility of every citizen." While talking within his comfort zone Victor's body had completely relaxed, relaxed enough for his face to resume a pompous expression, his trademark look.

"Get off your soapbox before I kick you off it. One day soon you can play professor to inmates. You'll be real popular in prison, they love egghead freaks who murder young women," said Estep.

"I had nothing to do with Lora getting killed!" Victor protested.

"Then how is it that the two of you were arrested together? You kept that tidbit to yourself, so what else are you lying about?" asked Estep.

Serena interjected at that point. She had been leaning against the wall; thinking about what she might add, and finally came up with what she thought was a good question. "What kind of work do you do, Victor?"

Victor looked at Serena in surprise. He seemed to have forgotten she was in the room. "Finally, someone who knows what to ask. You got it, it's Henry they wanted, and they got him. I don't know why they went after Lora, but if they got her, they were coming after me next."

"Who's Henry?" asked Serena.

Estep made a guttural noise in his throat to indicate his disgust, and his abrupt re-appearance. "It's his computer," he said.

"Henry and I spent years together. I still can't believe they took him. But I have Emily and that old gal will clear my good name," said Victor, his eyes tearing up again.

"Emily is…?" asked Serena, already having guessed the answer.

"Another computer," said Estep.

"That still doesn't explain the arrest. Why did you lie to Agent Estep about that?" asked Serena.

"It had nothing to do with this. What happens behind closed doors should stay behind closed doors!" Victor's face was flushed and sweaty.

"He was arrested for…?" asked Estep. He looked at Serena, not bothering to ask Victor directly.

"Lewd behavior in a public place," said Serena.

"That doesn't sound like closed doors to me," said Estep.

"Movie theater. And we were alone," said Victor.

"You were in a public place, which makes your right to privacy null and void," said Estep. He came close to calling Victor a few of his favorite derogatory names, but reigned himself in; a struggle that was evident to both Victor and Serena. After a moment of frustrated silence he addressed Serena. "I'll have my team fact-check, but it rings true to me."

"Yeah, I'm good. I don't think he's lying." The last thing Serena wanted was more details about the lewd behavior. "Well, not about that anyway. I think he had something to do with Lora and that bug."

"Of course he did! Weren't you listening? Our team asked him to set up the technology and outfit Lora with it," said Estep.

"Why didn't you brief me on that? I wasted my time reviewing and analyzing the audio file when you already knew everything. Were you deliberately giving me bogus work to keep me busy?"

Estep walked closer to Serena, turning his back on Victor. He looked down upon her from his towering height and said, "Yes."

Serena struggled to maintain her composure as she felt the heat of humiliation sweep across her face. "I get that you don't respect me, but can you at least let me try to help? Doesn't President Kinji's endorsement of me mean anything to you?"

"Yes, I respect the President. Point taken. Look, we both want the same thing here."

"Agreed." After a bit of reflection she went on to say, "So our biggest lead is with him, then?"

Serena looked at Victor, and then quickly averted her eyes.

"Yep, for now anyway."

Estep and Serena continued talking as if Victor was not in the room. "I hope it's obvious what the FYD wanted from his computer. Are we even sure it's really the FYD behind this?" asked Serena.

"No, we aren't sure. We haven't had time to dig into much of anything," said Estep.

"Of course it's the FYD. I met with them before!"

Estep and Serena whirled around to face Victor. Victor gasped and placed both of his pale hands over his grotesque mouth. "I said too much, didn't I?" he said.

Before Estep could lunge at Victor, Serena told Estep firmly, in her Mom voice, "I've got this – let me handle it."

She hated to pull rank, but a middle-aged woman with many years of experience in dealing with dramatic children trumped a young single male who had no experience with heading off meltdowns. No, Estep's specialty lay in the realm of hardened criminals and sophisticated spies. He was out of his league.

Serena swallowed her revulsion at having to get up close and personal with Victor, who, she quickly discovered, reeked of BO mixed with something else – Doritos? She tapped into her surgeon-like nerves of steel to propel herself forward until her face was mere inches away from Victor's pasty mask of comedy and tragedy. She stared into his cement-colored eyes with bird-like intensity: Victor was a piece of road kill and until the eagles and hawks took over, Serena would enjoy the first pickings.

"Tell me everything about your meeting with the FYD," said Serena.

Victor was taken aback: somewhere in his subconscious was the memory of his own mother's eerie green-sky warning before the tornado; the calm voice that was scarier than the punishment that would quickly follow if he didn't obey. He complied with Serena's order without hesitation.

Agent Estep looked both vexed and impressed. Serena squelched the urge to gloat as Victor began to spill what seemed to be the whole story, and beyond, if she was paying attention to Victor's embellishments.

"I was minding my own business, trying to

break into the app market. You know, get a good game in there, start out free then charge as much as the market will bear after the gamers are hooked. I was messing with the new codes and stumbled upon a slicker, faster language. I thought, why sit on my thumbs and let some other guy make millions off of my idea? It's a gold mine in apps and I was going to be the first panhandler to dive in with this new language, this newer, more efficient, pan so to speak. I went to the big money bakers and showed them what I had. Most didn't let me through the front door, but two of them did."

"Victor, as much as I love a good nerd story, get to the point," said Estep.

Victor placed his hand over his heart in a wildly dramatic gesture of offense. "Am I boring you?"

Estep grunted. His handsome looks were masked by his perpetually dark moods. He looked particularly ugly at the moment.

Serena tried in vain to think of an excuse to get Estep out of the interrogation room before he blew. She was relieved when Victor had the same idea.

Victor said, "I'm not saying another word until he leaves. From now on I'm talking only to you,

Miss…"

"Serena."

"Miss Serena." Victor smiled broadly. He looked almost charming.

Estep didn't put up a fight and he didn't waste any time heading out the door. And, as if his feelings about leaving Victor for Serena to deal with weren't clear enough already, he was finally smiling. Ah, there was that handsome face again, thought Serena.

Before leaving the room Estep said, "I want that when you're done." He tossed the recording device that he had been wearing all along, concealed, at Serena. She was not expecting something to be thrown at her. Fortunately her reflexes were sharp and she caught it before it hit her in the face. She puzzled over it a little while, and was about to ask Estep if she needed to turn it on or something, but he was already gone.

"Well, then, it's just you and me, Princess," said Victor.

"No more interruptions. I'm listening – take your time," coaxed Serena. She was aiming for the voice of an enchantress, slow and husky, halting, hypnotizing. Tell me everything, I won't hurt you, she imagined herself projecting.

"Is there something wrong with your eye?" asked Victor.

Serena dropped her attempt at bewitching Victor and said, in her normal voice, "No. Back to what you were saying about the FYD."

Victor asked for water, drank it all in one long gulping session, crossed his legs, folded his hands on one knee, then, after a bit more fidgeting and preening, he began his monologue:

"The FYD was created as a result of the increases in food prices which led to the decrease in gains, the reversal of gains, in poverty reduction. Take Africa. In 2008, food prices were getting alarmingly high. Food prices stabilized some, came back down – although not as big of a percentage of decrease in Africa – and then costs began to climb overall again. Of course after the big war, food prices were out of reach for the American poor, let alone the African poor. Anyway, rice, cereals, maize, wheat – all are imports out of reach for poor nations across the globe, not just Africa. But I mention Africa because they are a nation more vulnerable to unstable food prices. Am I losing you?"

"No, I think I've got it. Other nations can bounce back from fluctuations in food prices easier," said Serena, who was wondering where this was all going. How did they get onto Africa?

"Well…to work toward sustainable food security in Africa, the Bank established in 2008 the Africa Food Crisis Response initiative, AFCR."

"The Bank?"

"The African Development Bank Group is probably the correct reference, but basically the World Food Bank. The goal is to reduce food poverty and malnutrition, short term, and achieve sustainable food security, long term. The Bank provides low-interest loans, interest-free credits, and grants to developing countries. The list of what they finance is long. They invest in education, health, public administration, infrastructure, financial and private sector development, agriculture, and environmental and natural resource management. They don't foot the entire bill – they co-finance with the countries themselves, or with investors. It's complicated. But bottom line, we're talking millions, and billions, of dollars poured into these projects."

"Millions and billions of dollars. You have my

attention. Where's there's big money…"

"There's corruption. The African Development Group had as its goal to increase rice production, so high-yield rice would be ideal, yes? So they involved the private sector for food security and promoted agricultural research. The African Crisis Response Facility was established. There were five countries directly benefiting from the AFCR initiative, and its success was a model for many more such initiatives involving many more countries."

"And these countries were not directly benefiting, I'm guessing? They got off course, tainted by greed. The money didn't go to the impoverished nations, but instead lined the pockets of the private sector, or corrupt governments. Am I right?" asked Serena.

"Well, yes and no. The World Bank was still doing amazing things, and their goals were still admirable. But, yes, some of the growth of the WB led to a situation in which there were organizations without a watchdog. In those cases, there was a mixed bag of greedy government officials and greedy private individuals. Which leads me to my point: FYD, Food Yield and Development, was created to assist the Bank, but that never quite took off. The plan was for each nation to have their own FYD, so ours would be FYD-US, Food Yield and Development of the United States. And then the WFYD—"

"World?" Serena guessed. She was trying to hurry Victor along. She was also getting an acronym headache.

"Yes, the World Food Yield and Development would be a watchdog over all the others. To prevent corruption. And all would support the World Bank, and all its initiatives. It was thought that more government was needed, others disagreed. As usual, nothing was accomplished. We dropped the ball on this, if you ask me."

"So is this the part where you tell me what the FYD wants with you? And what do you have on your computer?" asked Serena.

"Henry," said Victor.

"Henry? Oh right, the computer. Go on," prodded Serena. She looked wistfully at the door.

"FYD would have, if they'd taken off, submitted statistics and pitches to the World Bank, to get funding. Like, for example, if research proved favorable on high yield corn, as I mentioned earlier in regards to poverty in Africa, well then, that could be a project selected for major funding," said Victor. He hesitated and looked around the room.

"What are you looking for?" asked Serena, even though she thought she knew the answer.

Victor didn't say anything. He gestured a writing motion. Serena gave him a pen and some paper. He wrote: "Walls have eyes."

Serena studied the sections of the room where she had seen Victor looking. Hmm, yes, there it is. A not-so-hidden camera. "While I get your concern, these are cameras. They can see you writing. So, how about you lower your voice and hope for the best? Besides, you're already detained. If you cooperate you'll get some leniency."

Victor whispered, "If I talk, we all die."

8

Ted was being watched. He could feel it. He felt it when he was awake; he felt it when he was trying to sleep. At night he tossed and turned so much that Ann had asked him on more than one occasion what his problem was. He wished he could tell her. He hated lying to his wife, who was also the President of his country. It was also hard, as the First Gentleman, to find time to be alone – how did he think he could get away with something like this? But he was going to give it his best shot.

Today was the day to go for it – everything was all set up and the green light to proceed had been given. It had taken him and his confidant over 48 hours to arrange. There was no way he wanted to jump through all these hoops again tomorrow; he vowed not to screw this up. Clandestine and absurd game-play was hard for a man who had enjoyed freedom for most of his life to accept as his new normal, but he would do what he had to do.

Ted went to McDonald's, which was not unusual. He stopped there for coffee occasionally. Sometimes he even had a Big Mac, which drew Clinton jokes from old timers from the D.C. days. Ted's secret service detail didn't think anything of it when his driver got into the drive-through line at a busy McDonald's on a Saturday afternoon. They followed him, of course, but Ted had anticipated that typical course of action.

Ted's driver ordered for Ted at the speaker – a small coffee only. They drove forward in the line. As Ted predicted would happen, the young agents in the car behind him had their mouths watered for burgers and fries. He waited until it was their turn at the speaker. When one of the agents was barking his order into the speaker Ted slipped out of his car, guessing that the agents would assume he had gone inside the restaurant to use the restroom.

Were they distracted enough by the busy drive through lane to let him go inside on his own? Ted resisted the urge to look over his shoulder. He kept moving, walking toward the restrooms. He didn't look behind him until a family with three kids filled the door frame. One of the kids was carrying a birthday gift bag, which came as no surprise to Ted, who had chosen this precise moment to come to McDonald's today -- the start time of a large children's party.

The party schedule for McDonald's was not difficult information to come by, and it was even easier than he had thought to hide himself in the chaos. The added bonus was that most of the kids and their parents were wearing paper hats that added more height and eye-clutter to the gaggle. His privacy barrier was even better than he expected!

By the time his agents drove around the other side of the building, he was already back out the same door he'd come in, where another driver was waiting for him – a driver of a non-government vehicle. Ted was confident that no one would have seen him walk back out, but he was not home free. His agents would be expecting him to come out the door near the drive through exit, where his regular driver was waiting for him, a driver who knew nothing of Ted's plans.

They'll go in there looking for me; I give them less than ten minutes. Probably closer to five. Ted hurried into the vehicle without drawing attention to him. He got in the back seat and reassured himself that the windows were tinted. Although it was unnecessary to do so, he couldn't resist saying, "Go!"

His new driver eased out of the McDonald's parking lot and into the congested street. Ted knew this area and had chosen it for its traffic patterns: fast moving, heavy flow, no traffic lights for a long stretch. As he had anticipated, the car Ted was riding in was quickly sucked into the flow, absorbed by Saturday shoppers and tourists. It was satisfying to look back and see nothing behind him that resembled a government vehicle. He was free!

And that was when his new driver pulled over, stopped, and turned around in her seat. Ted gasped. "It's you," he said.

"Yes, it's me. Did you really think that I

wouldn't know that you were hiding something from me?"

"I hoped," Ted said.

President Ann Kinji, aka Ted's wife, laughed. "Your first mistake was recruiting one of my friends. Of course she went straight to me and told me what you were doing."

"My secret service detail? They knew all along?"

"No, you fooled them. No one knows about this but you, me, and our mutual friend Penny."

"How did you get away from your detail?"

"I put Penny on the detail today. They are following us discretely."

"We can trust Penny."

"Of course we can, she's the one who told us that something was rotten in the Cube."

"Then we can proceed with the plan?" asked Ted.

"I don't know your plan. All I know is that you asked Penny to help you evade your security detail. Are you going to tell me what you planned to do?"

Ah, that explains it, he thought. She didn't know.

"I can tell from your hesitation that you are

wondering if you should tell me or not. Whatever it is, you know I'll find out eventually," said Ann.

"I know where Serena is," Ted said without fanfare.

Ann perked up. "Why didn't you say anything?"

"Because they are keeping it a secret from you, from us," said Ted.

"Who are they?"

"I don't know, but I'd like to find out. I don't think the President of the newly united States should be any part of this."

"And you should?"

"If not me, who? If something stinks in the Cube, I don't know where the smell is coming from. We have to trust someone though, and we do trust Penny. I assume we can trust her judgment in people too."

"Yes, my detail is sound," Ann confirmed. She felt no reservation in asserting her confidence – her intuition had never failed her before and she had no reason to doubt her God-given gift now. "Your plan was what? Go to where Serena is and fight all the bad guys yourself?

"Of course not."

"Then what was the plan?"

"I was told to meet with someone in a Gasthaus, and he would tell me everything."

"A Gasthaus? She's still in Germany?"

"Apparently."

"Why the cloak and dagger routine?"

"He said he was worried about the others knowing that he was meeting with me. I'm supposed to be there two days from now."

"How did you expect to stay away that long without anyone noticing you were gone?"

"I was going to tell you before everything hit the fan, but not until I was already on the plane. Besides, no one really cares what I do with my time as long as it doesn't reflect badly on you."

"I see. Your plan is severely flawed. First of all, you aren't meeting with him yourself. We have trained people for that."

"He specifically said that no one could be trusted. He made it clear that he wanted me to be the one he talked to, and given the compromised situation we have I agree with him."

"You know we never negotiate in these situations. It's ridiculous that the First Gentleman would be acting like an agent, and that you'd do something like this behind my back."

"This is why I didn't tell you. I knew you'd try to talk me out of it. Besides, I wanted to protect you. What you didn't know wouldn't have hurt you, but here you are."

"Yes, here I am. What else did he say? And how did he contact you in the first place?"

"He somehow got directly through to my private line."

"What? Who would let that happen? Follow that security leak and we will have a lead on where the stink is coming from. Anything else I should know about?"

"He said something about too many people knowing about 'Covert Coffee'. That mean anything to you?"

"Covert Coffee is my operation."

"Now you're acting like an agent."

"Of course not! My team is on this."

Ted reached forward from his position in the backseat to touch Ann's shoulder. He gave her a gentle squeeze and said, "Madam President, are you sure you know who your team is?

9

Paul didn't mind his prison life. It was oddly liberating. No longer the puppet of his deranged older brother, Paul was free in a way that transcended prison bars. Besides, he had The Social Media Channel to keep him company: the voices of the masses, plus millions of published digital books. He could feed his mind and spirit with no limits – with no job and no house to maintain he had all the time in the world.

All the social networking, reading, meditating,

praying, deep breathing, yoga, pottery, painting, and Zen gardening were clearly a big part of his therapy, but was only part of the transformative process. It was his spiritual awakening that was the most responsible for the man Paul was today. His life-changing epiphany: When one feels dead, there is nothing left to fear; how boundless life becomes!

Not content to keep such new-found wisdom to himself, Paul shared his secret to joyful living with anyone who visited him and in a series of self-help books that hit all of the important bestseller lists. His PR team had tweaked his now-famous quote to be more marketable: When one has no fear of dying; how boundless life becomes!

The book would have sold itself because naturally everyone was curious about what Paul, the man who blew up two American presidents, one former and one sitting, was thinking. Not that anyone mourned the loss of the two men who had perished under his hand: clearly the newly re-united nation was much better off without those misogynistic prigs. So, while Paul was a murderer and a terrorist, he was nonetheless an American hero according to The Social Media Channel polls, which Paul tuned into daily.

In fact, he never tuned out. The SM Channel was a television station devoted to a running stream of never-ending, seldom-slowing social media content. International, national, and state official tweets ran along the bottom of the screen like the old CNN tickertape. Opt-in and personal social media filled the main screen. Multiple users could view SM Channel together, a common situation in a household with a wide screen television, although most people hid their personal feeds when sharing a screen with others.

Paul, alone in his prison cell, had no such privacy concerns. He programmed his own name into his customized SM Channel settings so that he was always plugged into what people were saying about him. The SM Channel drew tweets, blogs, statuses, blurbs, messages, forums – all of it – everything out there, every and any social media, into one screen. Paul tracked several keywords, or tags, all at once. He even kept multiple screens open, like a picture-in-picture TV. Some of his screens were stacked in multiples. And yet he kept up with all of it.

Paul heard a ping on one of his tags. Interesting, he thought. Haven't seen that name pop up in a while. What's going on?

The ping signaled that Nicholas was active on the SM Channel. Nicholas was the young computer genius that his brother Clyde had recruited for the computer lab – the lab had been Clyde's baby, not Paul's, but regardless of ownership the lab was seized by the United States government even before cuffs were chafing Paul's hands. The news that Nicholas was apparently now working for Big Brother didn't surprise Paul in the slightest.

But what was surprising was that Nicholas was reaching out into Cyberspace to dig for information. Why would he do that when he had access to the best security technologically possible? The SM Channel had only consumer-level encryption. A hacker could crack that wide open in minutes. So why was Nicholas using it? Why, indeed.

Paul spoke into his SM Channel watch. Most households were given an SM Channel pen, gratis from the government. The argument for providing SM pens, known as "digi pens", to every household was the same as in the days of funding public television – every citizen should have access to information. All law-abiding Americans could access the SM Channel and cellular phone service via the digi pen, but inmates were not allowed to have such an instrument. They were issued watches instead.

Speaking into the watch was something Paul did every waking hour, a habit that grated on his fellow inmates' nerves. And yet, certain inmates listened to everything Paul said, hoping for a tidbit that would interest a reporter. After all, there might be a book deal to the hangers-on.

"Show me location," he said.

A map spread across the screen with a virtual pin over Hudson, Wisconsin. The pin lowered and the map zoomed in tighter, tighter, tighter, until Paul was looking right into the computer lab windows. He could see Nicholas at the window, as clearly as if he was doing a teleconference. Paul looked the kid over. Yep, that was the same kid. He had grown a lot since he had seen him last, but yes, that was him. Paul was about to zoom back out, but it was too late. Nicholas had apparently seen Paul's signal pop up on whatever security application he had been running. Ahah, so Nicholas was using secret and advanced stuff all along. This makes sense now.

Paul read the message on his screen a few

times, letting it sink in: PAUL – I SEE YOU! KNEW YOU'D BE WATCHING. THANKS FOR MENTIONING ME IN YOUR BOOK. I THREW YOU A SIGNAL, WANTED TO GET YOUR ATTENTION. NEED YOUR HELP, YOU IN?

What could he possibly need Paul's help with? Paul was intrigued, to say the least. He replied, speaking into his watch, "Count me in, what can I do?"

CAN'T KEEP THIS LINE SECURE FOR LONG. SM CHANNEL NOT THE BEST PLATFORM. SERENA ASKED FOR YOU. YOU CAN ASK HER WHEN YOU GET HERE. SORRY, HAVE TO DISCONNECT.

Serena? Serena Wilcox? She was the last person he would have expected to seek out his company. Last he knew Serena was personal friends with the president of the United States, President Ann Kinji. So this was big. Very big.

Paul did something he had not done for months: he turned off the SM Channel. Then he packed up the few belongings allowed in the cell, made his bed, and brushed his teeth. He was beginning to floss, with a tiny inmate-approved flossing tool, when he heard footsteps approaching his cell door.

10

President Ann Kinji absorbed her husband's words: "He somehow got directly through to my private line." She let her body sink into the plush seat cushion of one of three chair-and-a-half loungers in the presidential library, the incredible room custom built for her and completed just three weeks ago.

The room was rushed into production after Kinji was overheard referring to her new home as "The Cube". It was unacceptable that President Ann

Kinji, a heroine seeing the nation through the worst chapter in American history, should be unhappy. President Ann, a president so loved that she was often affectionately referred to by her first name, should have the presidential room of her dreams.

Private citizens worth millions, some worth billions, gathered in emergency fund-raising sessions; large gala events complete with paparazzi to cover them. Within a few short days the money was in the bank and the best architects in the world were hired. The entire project was brought from conception to finish in less than 18 months, a feat so incredible that Americans were inspired to believe that the new America had rekindled innovation reminiscent of the days when Walt Disney was still living, Virginia believed in Santa Claus, and Jimmy Stewart's George Bailey learned that it's a wonderful life.

And the result was sensational! The library was designed to look like an old vaudeville theater. The bookcases had the appearance of audience seating – rows and rows of books, spiraling up and up, to the highest heights where balconies were nearly flush with the glass ceiling. The stage area held a platform reading space with burgundy stage curtains framing the seating area. From the stage Ann could look out over her audience of books, books, and more books.

For no matter how many digital books she had downloaded over the years, she never gave up her love of holding a real book in her hands. These days, real books were like pieces of art: collectables. Not many people read printed pages anymore, and certainly few contemporary works were inked on real paper, but books themselves had never lost their beauty, or the power to calm her. Ann's library was the only place in The Cube where she felt at home.

While she had only had the space for a little over twenty-one days, she had already developed a daily habit of spending at least an hour a day in the library and she was firm about the rules regarding the new space. She banned The Social Media Channel from her library – no screens of any kind were allowed in. No gadgets, no digi pens, nothing. The intercom system was the only way to reach Ann when she was in her sanctuary, her resting place that literally did have a sanctuary, an incredible one.

The "audience" of books filled half of the

library's sphere, and the stage/set (seating area) was across from the audience, as expected if imagining the room looking like a traditional theater house. The space where an orchestra pit would be was the space set aside for Ann's sanctuary. Ann's design team had worked with her to create a prayer and reflection space in the center of the library.

The sanctuary was an indoor garden, both ingenious and beautiful. The entire garden was no larger than the imagined orchestra pit space – it was compact and space efficient. Every inch of it was utilized: pavers with mosses and flowering ground-cover between stones served as flooring; flower beds were arranged organically around the trellis, pond, and butterfly garden; retaining walls held fruit trees, berry bushes and a small assortment of vegetables. There was a lattice arch with flowering vines that created a canopy of blooms; climbing roses, morning glories, sweet peas, and more exotic vines like the "Double Blue Butterfly Pea Vine" and the "Chocolate Vine", a beautiful climber with distinct chocolate colored flowers that give off a slight hint of chocolate fragrance.

The exotic vines were zoned for tropical climates. Therefore the garden was kept quite warm, with a high level of humidity created by a system of over a hundred misters discretely hidden amongst the plants. Ann relished the warmth and anticipated the freedom of wearing sleeveless summer dresses even in the dead of winter, which would creep up on her again sooner than she cared to think about.

Even the library bathroom was planned by a team of designers. It was generously sized and included a luxury dressing room where Ann kept all of her favorite cotton clothing, mostly beach dresses and oversized T-shirts. She also stored a collection of straw hats to protect herself from the surprisingly harsh rays that blasted through the library's enormous skylight dome.

The center of the dome was above the heart of the garden where flowering vines created a focal point for water fountains, bird baths, and bird feeders – an attractant for the many beautiful song birds that resided in the garden. Other garden residents were Koi in the pond, butterflies in the butterfly garden that surrounded the pond, and helpful-to-plants insects such as ladybugs, found in largest concentration in the plants near the masterpiece sculpture fountain.

At the base of the fountain was a 2-person wrought iron bistro set, perfect for enjoying a morning cup of coffee. But Ann's favorite place to relax was under the flowering vines in a futon swing, the final touch to complete the enchanted garden. Overlooking the entire glorious display was the stage seating, where Ann was currently still slumped in a lounger.

As she looked out over her flowers, past the natural beauty of the gardens to the balconies of man-made books, a flurry of movement caught her attention. She smiled. Ah, a hummingbird was at the trumpet vine. She allowed herself to relax again – she was safe within her domed library, her enchanted garden. This really was a beautiful world that her people had created for her, their queen.

But as she had said in her speech on ribbon-cutting day, this multi-million dollar project dedicated to her by some of the world's most successful people in business and the arts "is nothing but a vulgarity if not repeated. Take this example of what can be done when the best of American ingenuity unites, and apply it to a project worthy of the best and brightest."

She challenged the Kinji Library &

Conservatory Foundation to adopt no fewer than ten of the neediest inner-city areas of the nation, ten of the neediest mid-sized towns, and ten of the neediest small towns. Reassemble the think tank. Generate funds. Bring back the galas, the red carpet, and the paparazzi. Make something beautiful. Use the triumphant library project, their new national treasure, as a shiny jewel to inspire something even more magical: something real, that would make a real difference.

Her speech was met with a standing ovation. The president of the Kinji Library and Conservatory Foundation stepped forward to say, "You make a real difference. You are worthy of something beautiful. I'm sure I speak for the entire foundation when I pledge to build upon what was started here today, and recreate America one community at a time." It took no convincing to get the team back together. They re-named themselves The New America Foundation and went to work planning a "re-building America's poorest" event that would make President Ann proud.

Yes, it seemed that the nation was headed into a wonderful era of healing and growth. And yet, here she was, worried about a rat in The Cube, an infestation that lingered from the previous administration and all the tragic events that preceded its hideous and shocking demise. Yes, there was leftover business to take care of.

And that was why Ann broke her own rules for the library, the sanctuary that she was now calling her enchanted garden: she brought in her digi pen. It was easy to smuggle in without notice. It was the size of a regular ink pen and no one would suspect that Ann, as vehement as she was about banning all technology from the Dome, would then herself bring in a gadget.

Before she used the digi, she took measures so that she would not be in view of the security cameras. She knew of one spot where the cameras could not focus on her. She sat on the swing under the floral cover, the plants having grown so lush that the view of her under the trellis was completely blotted out by blossoms, leaves, and vines. She breathed in the hint of chocolate from the Akebia quinata and steadied her nerves. What she was about to do was ridiculous. She was going rogue – no one in her cabinet, on her staff, not even the First Gentleman, would know what she was up to.

11

Former Special Agent Lehman felt the warmth of his digi pen through the fabric of his shirt pocket – he had set it to "heating mode", as it was quieter than vibrating mode. Because he wasn't expecting an urgent message, or any message for that matter, he took his sweet time reaching for the pen. Another bite to eat, another couple of sips of wine from a bottle of Barbera --his favorite Italian variety – then he'd look into who was trying to reach him. His time was his own! Why not enjoy the best benefit to being a private citizen?

His professional life after he left the civil service was quietly devoted to his lucrative career in the IT department of a well-known company, and while he was often on call, his assignments were hardly the emergency status or danger level of a covert mission. As for his personal life, what a change from lonely hurried weekends of his civil service days when he never had time to do much more than catch a movie – and when he did finally make it to the cinema he rarely got to stay to the final credits.

Now Lehman had plenty of time for leisurely pursuits. He scheduled week-long vacations on exotic beaches and regularly indulged in his new hobby: dining in new restaurants with his wife and later reviewing them for his blog. This was what he was doing right now – the dining part of his foodie lifestyle. Later he would re-live the experience by blogging it. Yes, life was good, and he didn't miss the fray of D.C. or the new digs in Chicago.

Nonetheless, when he saw the caller ID on the tiny digi screen, his pulse quickened. He slid his entrée, the Veal Osso Bucco, toward the middle of the table to use the table surface for writing.

Flustered, he dropped the digi pen twice before finally grasping it firmly. He wrote, "Madam President, I'm here."

Lehman's wife leaned over the table and mouthed, "Who are you talking to?"

Lehman whispered, "President Kinji." He resumed talking at a normal level, "There's a delay in transmission, I'm on hold."

His wife gasped. "What does she want? Doesn't she know you aren't an agent anymore?"

"I think so, yes, of course she does. She gave me a nice card when I left, remember? You said I should frame it."

"Then what does she want?"

"I don't know, she hasn't answer— wait, she's saying something," said Lehman.

He pulled the rubbery tab on the end of the pen to extract the digi ear bud. He inserted it into his right ear and listened to the message. "I need your help. In fact, I need a team outside of The Cube. Who can you find on short notice? People you trust, and no one active."

Lehman wrote with the pen, "You need me to create a team and head it up? What is the mission?"

"There's a, for lack of a better word, traitor in

the Cube. I don't know who, or how many. Something left over from President William's days and probably earlier."

"Can I talk to my wife first?"

"Of course."

Lehman's wife nodded vigorously when he brought her up to speed. "I know you'll do the right thing. I'm behind you," she said.

Lehman wrote: "My wife's here, gave me the green light. I can get a team together, but some of them had their security clearances revoked."

"That won't be a problem," said Ann.

"You have a location?"

"You'll be working at the lab in Hudson."

"The Minnesota lab?"

"We moved it to Wisconsin."

"Got it. When do I go?"

"There's someone outside waiting for you, about a block away from GianMarco's – that's where you are, correct?"

"Yes. You tracked me through my digi pen?"

"I don't know how they did it, I told them I wanted you found and they found you."

"No offense, Madam President, but you are on your digi. Did you disable the tracking feature?"

"Yes, I did. And I'm using the text-to-speech function, so my correspondence with you is silent."

"Cameras?"

"I'm concealed by flowers."

"Pardon?"

"By—Agent Lehman, I'm fine. Please focus on your mission. My people are waiting for you. It's a long way from Homewood, Alabama to Hudson, Wisconsin."

"Yes, I'm on my way."

"I knew I could count on you, Agent Lehman."

"Thank you, Madam President." He wasn't sure how heartfelt he was. Part of him was over-the-moon with pride that his President trusted him above anyone else she could have called upon, but another part, possibly a larger part, of him was sickened at the thought of leaving his wife and job, and all of Birmingham for who knows how long. Would everything be the same when he returned? Would he be the same when he returned?

12

Lehman's first move was to assemble his team. On the top of the list was "The Beav", one of the former agents he knew whose security clearance had been revoked – the biggest scapegoat on the chopping block when the flushing of the agency began. Beav was spectacularly tangled up in the mess with Paul and the most obvious choice to sacrifice first. He had been present when an explosion took down two American presidents with one high-tech bomb that had been disguised as a bugging device. Beav, the team's technology expert, had failed to recognize the device as a bomb even after he'd hand-inspected it.

Of course Beav had no way of knowing that Paul was capable of that level of violence, nor should any reasonable person hold him responsible for anything that transpired, but anyone even remotely connected to that tragic and highly-avoidable national disaster was swiftly fired with no hope of working in government service again; and Beav was directly responsible for botching the inspection of the device. While Lehman had taken an early retirement with honors –having escaped the firing sweep because he wasn't anywhere near that fiasco—poor Beav, one of the best agents Lehman had ever known, was hung out to dry. Lehman's jaw clenched in memory of the witch hunt. The nation demanded that people be held accountable and naturally the easiest place to start was with the little people, the ones who put their lives on the line for everyone else. Lehman wasn't sure what washed up condition he would find Beav in. Would he even be fit to serve?

The Beav answered Lehman's call on the first ring. His voice was unnaturally chipper which was his typical state of being, especially if he had been up all night on a creative bender, sans alcohol or any other substance. He revved himself up on mania alone, the ideas churning inside his head, silenced only when his project was complete. Whether it was an underground library bedroom, a butterfly garden, or building a series of walls – Beav would not sleep until he hit a stopping point, which often drove him to the brink of insanity. It was in this crazed state of sleep-deprivation that Lehman found him.

"I just got back from a run, and I'm on my way to the gym," said Beav.

"Can you see yourself boarding a plane to Germany instead?"

"I'm in the middle of a project. Beating myself up at the gym to stay alert. Then I'm back at it."

"What project? Who are you working for?"

"Nobody. Me. I'm making a spiral staircase for my bedroom library."

This was normal behavior, thriving even, for Beav. Yes, he had called the right man for the job. "Suspend the staircase plan for now. I need your help."

"Why Germany? Do they eat a lot of red meat

there?"

Lehman ignored the meat question. The Beav's aversion to meat was well-known and not an issue he had time for. "The President believes that Serena Wilcox might be held there."

"Against her will?"

"Of course, against her will." Lehman wished he wasn't holed up in his car. He had a desperate need to walk off his frustration. "You need to go there, find her, and bring her back."

"Alive?"

"What? Of course we want her alive!"

"No, I mean: Do you think she is alive?"

"I hope so."

"Who has her? What do they want with her?" Beav piled dirty dishes into the sink to rinse them off. He spoke loudly over the running water.

"That's for you to find out. You'll meet with a guy, go from there."

"A guy? A contact? He's expecting me?"

"He's expecting the First Gentleman."

"Got it. Anything else I need to know?" Beav wiped down the countertop and took a quick inventory of the house.

"Nope, I sent everything else to your phone.

Your flight leaves inside of two hours."

"Hey, bud, thanks for the gig."

"No problem. Beav? You know you can never be re-instated, right?"

"Off the books."

"To your grave."

"Got it. I'll be in touch. Auf Wiedersehen!" Beav grabbed a leather backpack from his closet, already packed with essential clothing, supplies, and food to last for three days, five if he was conservative. He kept it at the ready for the call he had known would one day come. And that wasn't all he kept ready: all those days at the gym kept him pumped, primed, and more ready than he had been when he was still in.

To keep his mind sharp he of course had his impressive library of mainly nonfiction books, an eclectic assortment. And sure enough, his mission strategy was already forming in his brain, yes, easy-please-y, as if he'd never stopped working. He told himself that he would be in and out of there in time to tackle the spiral staircase by the following weekend.

He got himself on the plane with plenty of time to spare. He settled into his seat, placed his buckwheat travel pillow around the back of his neck, and allowed himself to sleep for the entire duration of the flight to Frankfurt. He barely stirred, even when his fellow passengers were restless and noisy. Upon arrival, Beav was well rested and primed. He grabbed his bags, joined the stream of unloading passengers, and made his way into the airport.

Travel to Germany was not much different than traveling anywhere else in the world but Beav remembered the old days, before the fall of the wall, when German airports were intimidating, especially if you were landing in Berlin. Armed guards with machine guns strolled the corridors. It was intimidating even for those who knew the language and carried a weapon of their own.

Germany today was such a far cry from those days of a divided nation, something that Beav saw happening right before his eyes in the United States: division before healing. Sort of. It was also vastly different, of course. Beav continued to muse and ponder the state of his nation, the state of Germany, the state of the world. He almost missed seeing the man who was following him, almost.

Beav took a mental snapshot of the man who

was keeping pace with him on the other side of the walkway. He assumed he would turn up again, probably at his next destination: Geisfeld, a little village not far from Bamberg. It was quite a drive from Frankfurt to Bamberg, but Beav felt certain that his stalker would have no problem staying on his tail. Maybe he even had a team. Beav felt smug: he didn't need a team. More importantly, he preferred to work alone.

He drove the rental car to Geisfeld. He made few stops, but every time he did take a restroom break he saw a familiar Audi pull up shortly after him. He placed a bet with himself that the Audi would reappear in Geisfeld, and sure enough he was right. It turned up parked along a narrow cobblestoned street near the Edeka convenience mart. Beav assumed his stalker was now following him on foot so he headed to a public place, a nearby Gasthaus. He ordered only Pomfritz, fries being the only thing on the menu he was willing to ingest. He dug around in his bag for a can of tuna to eat from for his main entrée.

The German wait staff was already curious about this German-speaking man with an American accent and Romanian ethnicity sitting in their small village alone. What business did he have here? How did he know about this place? It wasn't listed in any tour guide that they were aware of. The Gasthaus was not only a restaurant serving typical German cuisine and pub style foods, but also served as a stable and arena for horses. Patrons of the restaurant could view the horses in their enclosed training arena via the glass windows that walled the dining space. Trainers led the beautiful animals into the arena to lightly exercise them and practice basic hurdles.

Was this mysterious American here for the horses, the food, or something else? Something else, the staff noted when another man joined the American at his table. The wait staff would have loved to have heard the conversation, but straining to keep up with English was difficult enough without competing with the din of the Fussball crowd who serendipitously entered the door at that moment. Besides, they had beer to pour – plenty of it!

The two men were satisfied that no one could listen in their conversation; there was no need to go to a more private location, and no desire. The Gasthaus was a good place to be on an evening that had taken on a wet chill. However, the two sat across the table from each other in silence. Beav held out for the other man to speak first. It was a long wait, but he won the battle of wills.

"I was expecting an American. I know it to be you," he said, with an accent Beav couldn't identify.

"You live around here?"

"No. I come for you."

"What do you want with me? Who do you think I am?" Beav spun his now-empty water glass like a toy top.

The stalker was briefly distracted by this. After a few seconds passed he said, "I know who you are. You are the one she sent instead of Mr. President. You take too many risks."

"I take risks?"

"America. America takes risks. I knew she wouldn't do what we asked." He fiddled with a coaster that had a beer logo imprinted on it.

"Then why ask it?" Beav was distracted by the perpetual motion of the coaster even though he himself had been spinning his empty glass only a minute before.

"We wanted her to send us a man she

believes."

"She believes?" Beav stared pointedly at the coaster.

The man lay the coaster on the table. "Not believes. Trusts. We expected she would send more of you."

"No, I'm it."

"You will do. I must work now."

"Work?"

"It is the time for telling you the reason we asked for you to come here."

Beav focused on what he went to Germany for. "What about Serena Wilcox?"

"No, she's not here."

"Then where is she?" Beav studied the man's face but didn't see any hint of guile. Nor did he seem threatening in any way.

"She's in the States. There is a computer center there. She is there, working for us."

"For the Germans?"

The man laughed. "No, not the Germans."

"Then who?"

"We are Supporters."

"Of?"

"President Ann Kinji, United States President

who sees beyond her own country."

Beav cut him off before the mysterious would-be kidnapper launched into a political rant. "Why did you lie to her about Serena Wilcox?"

"She thinks Serena is here, that is good. We keep her thinking that."

"Because?"

"The corruption is deeper than she knows. We will work quietly, give her a wild duck chase."

"Goose."

"What?"

"Never mind."

"We keep her thinking Serena is in Germany. We get her to send a man to us, someone who can help us."

"I follow you so far. But who are the supporters exactly, and what do you need from me?" Beav didn't think he looked like the militia type, but what did he know about who was the militia type? He wasn't a profiler or even an agent anymore.

"We are an underground of patriots who met on the SM."

"The Social Media Channel?"

"Yes."

"I don't follow."

"We are mathematics. We are from Uni. Not all, but many."

"You are computer programmers?"

"Among other things. Researchers." The man's eyes darted back and forth.

"And?"

He leaned across the table and whispered, his breath heavy with medical spearmint from antacid tablets. "And we saw something we weren't supposed to see. There was an exposure."

"An exposure?"

"A crack."

"I don't understand."

"We could see in." The man's eyes opened wide, as if he were seeing everything all over again.

"I am still not getting it."

"We saw that they were there. You have a name you like to say. 'Big Brother'."

"The government?" Beav wondered if this man might be militia after all. He feigned dropping the coaster under the table so that he had an excuse to dart forward to pick it up. His sudden lunge didn't faze the man at all. He didn't seem like a soldier, not even of the home-grown variety.

"Yes, your government was inside. It started with the organ donor registry, it was before the SM Channel put all the social media together."

"Yes, I remember." Beav slid an elastic band off of his wrist and used it to pull his hair back. He hadn't cut his hair since he left the agency.

"Then they matched with birth certificates and blood types." The man had a smooth style of speaking even though English was obviously a second language for him.

"Yes, that's how it generally works."

"No, they matched in system. Database on every citizen has blood type."

"Creepy I guess, but I still don't understand." Beav's fries were gone and so was the tuna he brought with him. While he was no longer hungry, he considered ordering more food because he was restless.

"They track people on SM."

"Right, that's not new information."

"They track through digi pen, through phone, through everything all going to same place – the SM."

"Yes? And?" Beav grabbed a menu and skimmed through it.

"They track keywords."

"Like a terrorist watch list?" Beav dismissed the idea of ordering any of the rich meats.

"No. They track everything said."

"I still don't see a problem here."

The man reached across the table and removed the menu from Beav's hands. "They block things they don't want said."

"Are you saying that our government is censoring what people are saying on the Internet?"

"Yes. Censoring. They stop people from hearing things they don't want your people to know."

Beav waited until the server filled his water glass and walked away before continuing. "Are you trying to tell me that the United States government, without the knowledge of our own president, is controlling the Internet?"

"Yes."

"How is that possible? Of course the Feds have been after backdoor access and 'wiretapping' for years, and have succeeded in some cases, but the SM is an international cooperative. Getting access would require agreement with other nations. Are you saying that this is a global takeover of the

Internet? If so, I find that hard to believe." Beav leaned sideways in his chair to see what the people in a neighboring table were eating.

"Some are working together with the United States."

"And their presidents don't know anything either?"

"I didn't say that."

13

Serena returned to the row of computers where Nicholas had been working. She expected to see him sitting exactly where he was when she left, but he wasn't there. Neither was her favorite hot-head Agent Estep.

"Where did everybody go?" asked Victor.

Serena studied Victor's expression. Was he calculating how quickly he could overpower her now that she was clearly alone? She would have reached for her back pocket to feign that she carried a gun, but she was wearing pocket-less loose-legging style comfort/yoga pants.

Out of habit her mind raced for an outwit-the-criminal Plan B, even though "physical response" was now a tool in her arsenal. How she was kicking herself for not reacting more quickly! Because, between the last case and this one, she had finally wised up; for nearly two years now she had been training heavily, attending Aikido class three times a week. Funny how she had completely blanked. The sight of Victor's clown face could make anyone lose their head, she consoled herself.

Her evaluation and (intended) reaction time took only a few seconds, but as she had anticipated, it was enough time for Victor to make his move. He bolted. He ran like a girl, even screaming while he ran. He made it to the doors but no farther. Like the entry, the exits were also secured – probably to prevent visitors from stealing data. Serena was grateful that the security system trapped Victor inside the lab. She didn't like to run. She also recalled the risk of a severed arm if caught by the snapping jaws of the door. The brutality of that possibility was nauseating to imagine.

She waited for Victor to decide what to do.

Surely he wouldn't attack her -- a realization that disappointed her a little. She had lost her window of opportunity to try her new Aikido skills in a real-life situation. She watched Victor as he searched for an exit. He looked like a giant guinea pig trapped in a cage.

"I can't get out."

Serena laughed. "I can see that. Nice try, though."

"I might as well help you."

"You might as well." She shrugged. "Can we get you started right now?"

"I want Henry."

"They took Henry. Will you settle for, what did you call the other one?"

"Who. Or whom."

Serena let that pass.

"Emily! Her name is Emily." He glanced around the computer stations for any sign of the mock iMac that Agent Estep's team had taken from his home. The system was already set up for him at a station he called his own without invitation. He marked his territory by pulling back the chair, plopping his butt onto the pleather seat cushion, and wheeling himself forward until his abdomen was pressed flush against the table. He booted up the computer, a process that took a surprisingly long time. While waiting for Emily to start up, Victor had a look on his face that reminded Serena of a dog in heat.

"I'll leave you two alone," she said.

"No, no, this will only take a minute. Pull up a seat." Victor made an air circle, an invitational gesture to have a threesome.

"I'm not into that sort of thing," she said.

"Huh?" Victor replied.

"Nothing. Go on." Serena shook off her revulsion. There was geek love, and then there was geek perversion. If ever a man had seriously fallen in love with a computer, it was Victor. If Serena could shudder on command she would have been shaking from head to toe to get all the willies off her.

"You won't believe the secrets Emily has inside her!"

"Oh, I don't need to know."

"What?" Victor spun around in his chair. His baffled expression made him look slightly less repugnant.

"Sorry, go on." Serena willed herself to focus.

"Emily has the facial recognition data for all of the FYD insiders. I can search via name, company title, role in project, anything, and watch this!" Victor typed in a name and the man's face popped up instantly.

"Who is that?"

"Oh that's nobody, an example."

"Can you pull up the data they wanted from you? What don't they want us to know?" Serena edged in closer while maintaining a big personal space bubble between her and Victor.

"I'm showing you. This, the facial recognition data, is one of the things they don't want you to know."

"But I don't get it. We can find that information through our own searches."

"No you can't."

"How so?"

"They hack their data, have been for as long as I've been involved."

"What do you mean? Have they assigned themselves a false identity?"

"Yes, using the IDs of dead people. It's old school identity theft, with a high tech way of doing it."

"How do you know this?"

Victor raised one enormous furry eyebrow. "Because I helped them do it. Who else would have the mad skills?"

Serena sensed she had offended him, but didn't have time to waste soothing his raw nerve. "Do you have record of this?"

Victor made a sputtering sound with his sucker-fish lips. "Surely you jest!" He punched in a few numbers and an impressive table appeared, complete with color coding. He had placed all the legal birth names on the X axis and the false identities, complete with photographs, on the Y axis. Several of his clients had over a dozen aliases. He scrolled down the first few pages.

"Stop! I recognize that couple." She pointed to the husband and wife duo on the screen. They were average looking, neither thin nor fat, neither ugly nor beautiful, neither light-skinned nor dark-skinned. They were forgettable and unremarkable in every way. She remembered seeing them in person, and even their height was average.

In Serena's mind, a dramatic outward appearance gave her a head's-up: this was a person to watch. Heavy or lean; tall or petite; hair in shades of raven, red, streaked, or blonde; tattoos and piercings, unusual facial features (a clown face for example, she thought as she looked at Victor), all of these were neon signs. Good or bad, such people were interesting and noticed. It was the average who blended into the fabric of society like a chameleon; it was the average she trusted least of all.

"They are Marci and Erik Chapman," said Victor.

"The names don't ring a bell, but I know I've met them. I'm having a hard time placing where."

"A fund raiser?"

"No, I'm not on the A list. I don't get invited to things like that."

"You are a personal friend of the President."

"Which hasn't boosted my status much."

"No, that's not what I meant."

"She doesn't expect me to join the political scene, it's not my world."

"Again, not what I meant."

"I could continue to try to guess what you meant, or you could just tell me." Serena had awareness that she was clenching her jaw; a habit that she knew from experience would bring on a stress headache unless she relaxed her jaw muscles.

"Regardless of your A-list snub, you probably met them."

"Where?"

Victor made a huffing sound of superiority. "They are on her staff. Do you watch the news? Follow SM Channel? Do you keep your eyes open when you walk the hallowed new-construction halls of the Cube?"

Serena ignored his jabs. "This makes no sense to me. These two are easily recognizable, by everyone but me apparently, even though neither of them looks anything but ordinary. So what good is changing their identities if people already know their faces?"

Victor apparently found her comment worthy of two hairy eyebrows because he raised them both and held them high on his pale forehead long enough that they began to quiver. "Think about it, you'll get there."

Serena nodded. "They change their faces."

Victor released his eyebrows. "Easy enough to do with latex. I programmed the template myself."

Serena sucked in a big gulp of air. "Got it now! You were jazzed about the facial ID data because you use it to create new faces!"

Victor made a trigger gesture with his hand, pulled the trigger and clacked his tongue, ending the routine with a slow wink of the eye. "No matter how much in the public eye, no matter how famous the celebrity or politician, everyone can go dark."

"And yet, with the right face, can still access secured areas. I can see where people would not want this information to see the light of day."

"Especially those who live a secret life of crime."

"And you know who these people are?" Serena prodded again.

"More than you realize." His clown-like grin hit a sinister level that was less Bozo and more IT.

"Care to explain?" Serena concealed a shudder.

"I told you, the FYD. They want my data."

"But why? What does Food Yield and Development want with this?"

"I'm not saying anything more in this place."

"Victor, you already mentioned FYD, you're already in deep. Tell me the rest of it."

"You're right. Cat's out of the bag now anyway. I said Marci and Erik's names aloud. I'm screwed."

"We are protecting you."

"You're joking, right? You can't protect me from them."

At that moment, the door to the lab opened. In walked an unlikely cast of characters, some of whom Serena recognized. At the front of the pack was Nicholas, who made a beeline for his computer. Bringing up the rear was a petulant Agent Estep. In the clutch was former Agent Lehman, the Beav, four other men Lehman chose for his team (unrecognized by Serena), and one last figure that astonished her.

Not much took Serena by surprise, but this blew her mind. What possible explanation could there be for Paul to be walking through the door in front of her? The answer would have to wait because Paul's grand entrance was interrupted by the sudden onset of gunfire.

14

Serena's ears felt like she had jammed cotton balls deep into her ear canals. For a few minutes she couldn't hear a thing. Her brain slowly processed what happened while the silence swallowed her. She stared in disbelief at the body slumped beside her. Then she screamed. It wasn't a prolonged girl-in-jeopardy kind of scream; it was more of a just-saw-a-rodent siren.

When she pulled herself together she said, "I should have known that his clown face wasn't real."

"It never occurred to me either," said Estep.

Serena pointed to her ears. "I can't hear you."

The two looked at the clown-faced man on the floor. His fat suit had slipped during his fall and was now twisted up around his hips. In the craziness Serena had somehow ended up with his latex face mask in her hand. She studied it, impressed with the quality and craftsmanship of the piece.

There was no need for any of them to hurry. Bound by his own disguise, Victor was not going anywhere. Of course they knew now that his name was not Victor. The man at their feet was easily recognizable as Erik Chapman, the very man that "Victor" had told them about. So many questions, so very many questions! But Serena's temporary deafness was too big of an obstacle. She stepped aside to let Estep sort out this bizarre situation.

Estep ushered everyone into the computer lab, guiding the group past Erik. He gave Nicholas a gentle push toward Serena, who caught on quickly that he was her charge. He led everyone else to the back of the room where a large conference table was the obvious destination. No one said a word as they obediently took a seat around the table. Estep orchestrated the entire transition without uttering a single word.

Once seated he broke the silence. "Pick him up and wheel him over here." He addressed no one in particular so at first no one moved. Realizing that no one was likely to volunteer, Estep leveled his gaze on the youngest man at the table who then bolted out of his chair and retrieved Erik. Everyone waited for Erik to be settled at the table, hands cuffed to the arms of the chair with two different sets of handcuffs.

Serena took the last remaining chair. "Nicholas' mother is coming to pick him up. We can muddle along without the child genius. He's seen enough action for one day."

"Agreed. Let's piece this together, shall we?" said Lehman. He surveyed the room in an exaggerated mime-like fashion: pausing as he examined each face. Estep was at the head of the table, with Serena on the other end. Between them, clockwise from Estep, was Lehman himself, Beav, Paul, and the most academic member of Lehman's team Agent Hodgson. On the other side of the table, counter-clockwise from Estep, was Erik, bound to his chair, and the remaining three former agents on

Lehman's team, two men and a woman, who had been mainly recruited for muscle.

Serena got the ball rolling. "I recognize most of you, but there are a few of you I don't know. More importantly, why are all of you here? This is an odd group. Why is Paul here? I assume you are in charge of this, Agent Lehman? Does that mean that Ann, President Kinji, has ordered this meeting?"

Estep snorted, "Are you done talking? I'd like to hear him talk." He jerked his head toward Lehman.

"I'm former-agent Lehman. I work for the private sector now. In fact, none of my team is currently in service, but all are all former agents. Yes, President Kinji asked for me to assemble a team. Why is Paul here? I have no idea. How we all managed to show up at the lab at the same time, I don't know that either. Your turn." He looked at Estep.

"Paul was picked up by my team. Serena, you should know, you asked for him," Estep scowled.

"I did not! I had nothing— oh. I may have mentioned to Nicholas that I could use Paul's help," Serena said.

"He took you at your word. He sent up a bat signal," said Estep.

"Do you need me or not? Why am I here?" asked Paul.

"Do you know how many strings I had to pull to get him out of prison? If you don't need him, I'll pull more strings to get you back in there with him," Estep threatened, no jest intended.

"No, no, I actually do need him. I didn't expect to have him here at my request, but yes, I do need his help," said Serena.

Lehman stood up to stretch his legs, which also put him in a position to command the table. "Before you get into that, which may or may not have anything to do with what I'm here for, I want the play-by-play on what went down. We have a man in a clown suit cuffed to a chair who happens to be a familiar face from Chicago. Why was he shooting at us?" Lehman looked across the conference table at Erik. "I'd ask you directly, but I'm fairly certain I wouldn't get an honest answer."

Beav was quick to respond, "Thank you for slamming him to the ground. Saved us from taking a hit, although he isn't much of a shot. I want answers too. This thing has fired up into a hot mess."

"What I want to know is how he got a gun in here," growled Estep at no one in particular. His team was still sitting in the sedans parked outside the lab. How they all missed a weapon, no matter how concealed, was a question Estep knew he would have to answer, and every word out of his mouth would be added to his permanent file. Unlike the others, Estep was still an active agent and he wanted to keep it that way. Everyone else could get sloppy or forget about protocol, but Estep had to watch himself or he too would end up on the team of rejects, or worse yet, assigned permanently to Serena Wilcox.

"Paul's presence is accounted for. Ditto for Agent Estep. The rest of you are all with former Agent Lehman – a team formed at President Kinji's request. You all showing up at the same time was a coincidence?" asked Serena.

"No, one of my agents phoned in that there were two unknown vehicles on route to the lab. We were already here, but I waited until Lehman's team pulled up to come inside," said Estep.

"And Nicholas? Why was he with you?" asked Serena. "He's gone now, by the way, I heard him leave."

"If you must know, I took him out for ice cream. He's fine," said Estep.

"You surprise me Estep. Sorry, it's hard to turn off the mother in me. Speaking of, when do I get to see my kids? President Kinji obviously already knows about me being here, so I'd like you to bring my family to me."

"She doesn't know you're here," said Lehman. "I didn't know myself until just now."

"I knew you weren't in Germany, I was just there," said Beav.

"Why were you in Germany?" asked Serena. "Looking for me? And why doesn't she know I'm here?"

"Yes, looking for you. Well, it's complicated," said Beav.

"All of this can wait, let's get into why Erik was shooting at us and why he was in a costume – what was he anyway, a clown?" asked Lehman.

Nine pairs of eyes zeroed in on Erik. But Erik said nothing. In fact, he didn't move at all. Not even his eyes. Slowly his mouth began to quiver as white foam bubbled up and spilled over his lips. His eyes rolled back into his head and his body convulsed violently. Everyone watched helplessly as their captive choked on his last breath.

"Great, now what!" said Serena. "Now we won't get anything more out of him."

"He wasn't going to talk to us anyway, that's why he did that to himself," said Lehman.

"Or maybe he didn't want to go to prison. It really doesn't matter why he did it. Either way, he's of no use to us now." Serena puffed her checks out and slowly exhaled.

"Search him," said Estep.

"I'm not touching him," said Beav. "And neither should anyone else. Trace amounts of whatever poison he took could transfer from him to us, through skin to skin contact. Honestly, I'm not jazzed about breathing the toxin either, especially since we have no idea what it is."

"How is it that none of us were watching him?" Serena complained to no one in particular.

Estep answered her anyway. "For starters, he jacked us around so much that I couldn't look at him without wanting to kill him myself, and I still want my job –no offense Beav. Secondly, why would any of us want to look at him?"

Everyone stared at the hideous creature still

bound to the chair. Serena got up. "I'm going to roll him over by the door and call 911."

"For someone so smart, you are the ditziest woman I've ever met. You can't call 911. This is a covert operation," Estep said.

"Then call someone. None of us want to touch him," said Serena.

Lehman took out his digi pen to make the call.

"No, no! Don't turn that thing on!"

"Keefer, what aren't you telling me?" asked Lehman.

"Carla Keefer, as in the Agent Keefer in Lora's files?" asked Serena.

"Former agent. I was let go without explanation," said Keefer.

"She was my pick. I recommended her to Lehman," said Beav. "She came to me after she was terminated and my gut told me she was fired because she saw something she shouldn't have. Tell them what you told me."

Keefer began, "When Lora was investigated, for a supposed routine security check of flagged Town Hall messages, I was given the instruction to leave the room. I didn't think anything of it because I don't generally get an invite to the interrogation room. While I was waiting I ducked into the restroom, figuring I had plenty of time to return before they needed me. It was out of order and normally I would have turned around and left, but I, well, I really had to go, so I ignored the sign and walked in anyway. There were three people in there, and none of them female. They stopped talking when they saw me. I was fired before the end of the day."

"Did you know the men you saw in the restroom?" asked Serena.

"Oh yes, it was, well, the dearly departed Erik Chapman," said Keefer. She paused. Everyone looked at the dead man during an awkward moment of silence. "And the other two were not regular to The Cube, but I had seen them with Erik enough to know who they were."

"And they were?" asked Serena.

"Agent Browning and Victor something-or-other, a scientist I think. Agent Hodgson would know, she's the brain." Agent Keefer folded her arms across her chest, effectively concluding her presentation.

At this point everyone started talking at once, including those who hadn't chimed in before.

When the babble subsided, Serena asked, "Does the real Victor look like a clown?"

"Oh yes, because that's what's important to know," scoffed Estep.

"You mean like Erik does, er, did?" asked Keefer.

"Yes, does Victor look like that at all?" asked Serena.

"No, not really. Victor is an ordinary looking guy I guess. Wait, I know where to find a picture of him," said Keefer. She typed in a few words on her phone. "See? This is him. Don't worry, this is my photo archive, I'm not sending a traceable signal." She held the phone up for everyone to look at.

"How is it that you had no idea what Victor looked like?" Serena asked Estep. "This guy looks nothing like the parody of a man that Erik was passing off as Victor."

"And how is it that you didn't know he was in prison?" asked Paul.

"What do you mean?" asked Lehman.

Paul had everyone leaning toward him, bodies hovering over the table, ears straining for his voice, just like the old days when he was able to command a room. He savored the moment. Then he spoke.

"He's a member of the Criminally Insane club, of which I am of course also a member. I know they fetched him from time to time, rumor was that he went to The Cube, but I didn't believe it. Apparently it was true. I didn't know his name, he answers to 'V'. He's brilliantly daft, always mumbling numbers and equations. As you can imagine it's not all that possible to socialize while in the booby hatch, but they do let us mingle on occasion. He stumbles about, drawing in the air with his finger like he's lecturing from a blackboard he sees in his head."

"No, that can't be right. The Victor I know looks and acts like a normal person," said Keefer.

"He can fake the funk when he has to. I've seen him snap right out of it, and act completely normal," said Paul.

"What is he in prison for?" asked Serena.

"That's easy to check," said Lehman.

There was a bit of commotion as everyone started to move at once, followed by the collective thought that, although they were in a computer lab with more than enough computers for each person, there was no need for all of them to look up the information. They settled on giving the task over to

Lehman who had originated the suggestion.

"Why is it that none of us know anything about Victor? If he committed an unspeakable crime, wouldn't we all know about it?" asked Serena. "Surely you in government circles would know something, but even I would know. It would have been on the news, the SM Channel."

"I wouldn't be so sure about that," said Beav.

"What do you mean? What do you know that I don't? We have to compare notes on everything," said Serena.

Estep laughed. "Oh, you're leading this operation now?"

Beav was the next to stand up, deliberately creating a noisy ruckus with his chair as he did so. Quietly, and in a dramatically even tone, he said, "Someone has to."

Next, Estep was on his feet.

Lehman was the voice of reason. "Really? We're going to turn on each other? Isn't this display of testosterone cliché?" He remained standing, but gestured for the two men to sit back down.

Estep and Beav stared each other down, but they obediently took their seats without a fight. Serena, however, was the next to pop out of her chair. She was not imposing, in her under-five-two glory, but nonetheless she had their attention.

"I've been thinking about Erik. Why did he portray Victor in such grotesque fashion? I'm not talking about the clown suit, although that is bizarre of course, and it speaks to contempt, which is what I'm getting at. Erik invented an entire personality for Victor. You should have seen what Estep and I were dealing with! He carried on about naming his computers, he was lustful toward them."

"Lustful toward what, the computers?" asked Agent Hodgson, speaking for the first time.

"Yes, it was weird, like a fetish. He also went into a story about his pet turtle being flushed down the toilet."

"Wait, back up to the computer fetish," said Hodgson. She stared intently at Serena with her blue eyes.

Serena was surprised by the intensity of Hodgson's attention. "Are you saying that Victor is a freak? Erik was portraying him correctly?"

"No! Not at all. I'm saying the opposite. Victor is a reserved person, an introvert. He likely has Asperger's. He would never act in such a way that would give an impression of deviance. He's also not capable of anything remotely flamboyant or sexual. His body language is like that of a turtle, barely in motion," said Hodgson.

"Sounds like you respect him. Is he a colleague?" asked Lehman.

"Yes, sort of. I've admired his work and I've been fortunate enough to observe him while he was involved in a think tank. He's not anything like what you are describing."

"You mentioned a turtle. Remember that I mentioned Erik, while pretending to be Victor, cried over a flushed pet turtle? Did he have a turtle?" asked Serena.

"No, not that I'm aware of. But his nickname was Turtle, for the reason I said. He moved methodically, slowly. He showed little emotion. He did care only for his computers, but lust is not a word I can imagine in the same sentence with Victor," said Hodgson.

Serena smiled. "Then I think my theory is correct. Erik's portrayal of Victor was so over-the-top and nasty, that it screams anger. He wasn't content to use Victor's identity; he wanted to degrade him too. The turtle flushing really clinches it. And furthermore, Erik was arrested for doing something perverse while pretending to be Victor! So my question is, why? What did Victor do that would inspire such resentment?"

"I didn't realize you had a PhD in Psychology," said Estep.

"I don't," said Serena.

"My point exactly," said Estep. "This is going nowhere. Also, the real issue is that law enforcement relied on security scan to verify Erik's ID. If they'd checked him out, Erik would have been caught way back then."

Lehman stepped in. "What else would you have expected them to have done? Security scans are usually accurate."

"What was he working on?" Serena ignored the Estep-led tangent into a blame game that couldn't end well.

Hodgson was quick to respond. "He was working on the very issue that Beav talked about, the crack. He had a solution for sealing the crack and preventing it from being penetrated in the future. Of course at this time, I didn't know that we had this big of a problem, but everyone was aware of a few hackers here and there. Victor had the answers and was promising the patch by the end of the month."

The Beav leapt out of his seat. "Thereby shutting down Erik's access to the Dark Side!"

Estep was the next up on his feet, targeting his glower on Hodgson's pretty face. "And you didn't think that something like this would be important for us to know?"

"No, I didn't think of it. I suppose it should have occurred to me, but I didn't connect the dots. Well, not until Serena asked the right questions," said Agent Hodgson, a woman Serena appreciated so very much at that moment, especially when she thought she saw tears in Estep's eyes.

15

President Ann Kinji was busy with tasks worthy of presidential attention and even the real and present danger of a possible assassination attempt was not enough for her to abandon her post. After all, every day was a day when assassination was possible when one was sitting president of the United States of America! Fortunately nothing unusual was planned besides the typical ebb and flow of The Cube; meetings, conference calls, briefings, and documents demanding her signature.

One of the first things she did when she became the first elected president of the newly reunited post Big War States of America was establish a new style of governing. Ann Kinji would not be campaigning during her presidency. She would not be vacationing. The honor of the office was worthy of sacrificing her own ambitions and personal life for the years she was in office. Some argued that retreats are a mental health issue, with the loudest voices coming from Congress, in defense of their own frequent vacationing schedule, but that was what her garden was for – and yoga, eating well, and her alone time with God. She centered herself without abandoning her post, as many hard-working Americans must do. No, she told her staff, vacations are a luxury that the President of the United States should give up while in office.

She fully expected her precedent to be knocked down; probably as soon as the next administration, but she hoped that her example would inspire future American presidents to at least cut back on how long they stayed away from The Cube. Having come from humble beginnings, Ann was aware of what message luxury vacations sent to Americans who were struggling to pay the bills: Their president didn't care about their problems, but instead flaunted his/her wealth! Not during Ann's term! Ann was "for the people", a campaign now restricted to free publicity only.

Yes, Ann was idealistic. And incredibly, unbelievably popular. Some predicted she would be assassinated, and Ann surmised that those who held this opinion would feel validated when the truth about Covert Coffee eventually, and inevitably, leaked out. Others predicted she would be run over by her own party, by lobbyists, and by all the insiders to the Cube leftover from the pre-Big War days on the Hill. Yes, Ann would be blindsided they said.

Ann concluded that both schools of thought were correct, which was serendipitously verified by an urgent message from Agent Lehman:

<<MADAM PRESIDENT, I'M SORRY TO REPORT THAT YOUR SUSPICIONS WERE CORRECT. YOU NEED TO MEET WITH ME, URGENT. THE LOCATION YOU SENT ME TO IS NO LONGER SECURE. PLEASE ADVISE.>>

No longer secure? How had that happened? The computer lab in Hudson, Wisconsin was top secret, hidden inside the walls of a luxury home near Willow Creek State Park. Experts insisted that the location would be secure for many years to come. How could it be compromised its first year in operation? This was a blunder to the tune of billions of dollars! First matter at hand was the immediate problem of where to meet with Lehman, and she realized that she couldn't meet with him herself. The cloak and dagger routine, as Beav had so boldly suggested, was ridiculous. She was President of the United States, not a member of Scooby-Doo and the Gang, although she did make a decent Velma with the right wig and glasses; her entry in a residence hall costume contest had won her a free pizza.

She called upon the only person left she could trust: the First Gentleman. Ted was the first man to ever hold that title and she was so proud of how he had defined the position. Ted didn't read stories to school children, even though he, of course, respected teachers and nurturers. He felt that his unique position in The Cube allowed him the opportunity to fill in the gaps. He wasn't a co-President, that would be a ridiculous exaggeration, but he was definitely a valuable asset to the presidency. He was with Ann most of the time, especially when the Vice President was required to be in a separate location from the President, as dictated by security or because the VP had a full agenda elsewhere.

Ann considered Ted to be her acting VP, her right hand man, something she knew her actual VP Morgan Canon was well aware of. Morgan was second chair and he was usually somewhere else. She realized with a start that she didn't really keep track of where he was half the time. She relied on her staff to do that. She didn't need him, fetch him, or otherwise engage in anything to do with him unless forced to do so by the schedule. Truth be told she had wanted someone else, a young governor by the name of Carson Landon who had an excellent track record for keeping his campaign promises. Morgan Canon was not only not her pick, but she was opposed to him altogether; his flip-flopping on issues made him untrustworthy.

What exactly did Morgan do now that he was VP? Was he the source of the stink in the Cube? How could she have been so stupid? Uh oh, this is the moment when Velma knows who the man under the mask is but he's still out there, hovering about, lurking behind every corner!

Naturally her thoughts turned darker and more accusatory. Before meeting with Lehman, or rather asking Ted to do it, shouldn't she arrange for a private chat with Morgan Canon? Ann fact-checked her runaway thoughts: Was this the part in the horror movie when viewers shouted, "Don't go in there alone!" or was she paranoid?

She dismissed the thought that she could be in real physical danger if she met with Morgan alone. Secret service detail would be outside the room. She wouldn't eat or drink anything he offered her, so certain was she that Morgan was corrupt and, as crazy as it sounded, he might resort to trying to get rid of her. It was simply too obvious. He had to be the one! Who else had that much power? The list of people who had insider information and could work behind her back without her knowledge was short.

She set the wheels in motion to meet with Morgan within the hour, face to face. And what a face that was! Morgan was not known for his good looks. He had a face like a ferret: narrow eyes set close together; a nose like a rodent's, long and sharpish; facial hair that lay short and fuzzy on his skin; coloring in browns and grays. Even his skin tone seemed gray.

Morgan was quick to agree to a meeting, so quick that she suspected he had been waiting for the call. He was in her office within ten minutes, a speed most impressive given that The Cube was a labyrinth of halls, rooms, and entire buildings. Like the Pentagon of glory days gone by, it was like a city within a city. How was it that Morgan was in the neighborhood when her staff called him?

And that was her first question. "How did you get here so fast, where were you?"

Morgan screwed up his eyes, now barely visible slits on a face even furrier than Ann remembered. "I was on my way to your office."

"You have something to discuss?" Ann let her skepticism show.

Morgan sniffed. "I see you won't be bothered to hide your doubt. Has our relationship sunk so low that we cast aside any attempt at social niceties?"

"Morgan, I never wanted you on my ticket, you know that. We've never been able to see eye to eye, and we haven't even seen each other period for weeks now. That's a bizarre President-VP relationship I must say."

"That's what I wanted to discuss with you. I have been advised of your upcoming schedule and I plan to be a part of it."

"Which part?"

"What do you mean?" Morgan was either truly baffled or a mighty fine actor.

"The backstabbing part? The traitorous part? The serpentine part? Or how about the 'liar, liar, pants on fire' part?"

Morgan's mouth dropped open.

"I suggest you close your mouth before your forked tongue rolls out."

"How dare you!"

"How dare I what? Have an honest conversation?"

"What exactly are you accusing me of, Madam President?"

"This is you fishing around to see what I know. Well, you've caught yourself an old shoe."

Morgan blinked.

Ann clarified, "I'm not telling you what I know."

"I know what old shoe meant."

"But you'll tell me what you know, now."

Morgan crossed his arms and shifted his

weight onto his heels. "You won't like what I have to say."

"We have about five minutes. We, our nation's president and vice president are currently in the same room together, doing nothing whatsoever to benefit mankind. I can't imagine that this is what the American people voted us into office for."

Morgan didn't hesitate. "It's Ted."

"Excuse me?"

"You heard me. Ted, the First Gentleman, your husband. Think about it, it makes sense. He is more of a VP than I am, don't you think I've noticed?"

"Then he already has what he wants. He has no motivation."

"No, he hasn't gotten what he wants."

"Which is?"

"Your job."

16

"Ah, the familiar smell of erasers with a hint of hotdog," said Serena. No one acknowledged that she'd said anything as the five of them (Estep, Lehman, Beav, Paul and Serena) walked the halls of Leesburg Elementary, a midsized public school in the Hoosier state.

Leesburg had been selected for a Presidential visit because Ann Kinji was from Warsaw, Indiana. Leesburg was one of several schools in the Warsaw community school district, and was not in any way connected to big money or politics. This school visit had been scheduled over a year in advance: a quick visit with school children followed by a Q&A session with the media to promote the new educational reforms that Kinji was pushing.

Local media was present and incredibly excited, each journalist hoping for their big break. National media was of course also in attendance, although the numbers were small compared to coverage for briefings on health care reform or the proposed tax reduction bill, but international journalists were sitting this one out altogether. Overall, it was a low-key event receiving little attention. All eyes were focused on events scheduled for later in the day; when Kinji was due to meet with the leaders of several oil-rich nations to discuss the GOB (Global Oil Bank) initiative. In addition, there was a professional sports press conference running at the same time as Kinji's grade school event. It was a no-brainer which one the public cared more about.

It was under this cloak of relative obscurity that Kinji arranged to meet Lehman and his cast of unlikely characters at Leesburg Elementary, right under the noses of the media and a community full of people who turned out for the event. After Kinji's Q&A session she did a mock good-bye drive past the parade of school children and their parents, and the reporters who were covering it all while impatient to head back to their respective stations. The children, now joined by the local junior high and high schools as well, waved flags at the presidential detail. They raised the flags higher when her limo passed by; accompanied by cheers, jumping around like popcorn, and screaming at volumes that could break glass. Then her driver pulled into an undisclosed location airstrip. From there they jumped through several hoops before doubling back to Leesburg Elementary where Lehman and crew were waiting for her in the school cafeteria.

The entire ruse was much more involved than one might expect, since far too many people knew of Kinji's plans. She couldn't pull off a clandestine meeting with former agents and Serena Wilcox without an elaborate plan. What the media, and even most of her security detail, didn't know was that there were two undisclosed locations. The real one was where Kinji got into a non-government issue vehicle, driven by her loyal friend Penny, who had been unofficially re-instated as her driver.

Penny circled back to Leesburg Elementary and drove so close to the building as to be parallel to the door on the passenger's side. Kinji quickly and easily exited the car and entered the school through the small maintenance door. No one was the wiser, although it took some sleight of hand to manage fooling her security detail up to that point.

Penny hand-picked a trustworthy driver on duty for the president's vehicle and hired a Kinji look-a-like to ride along at all times. The look-a-like stayed out of sight while the real president was in the vehicle, and then slid into Kinji's vacant seat when Kinji exited. A semi-truck driver was also in on the charade: he parked his truck strategically for enough seconds to allow Kinji to exit the vehicle unnoticed by her security detail. The whole exchange took place at a rest stop and couldn't have gone more smoothly. From there, they journeyed on to the decoy location where the President's jet was waiting.

The plan was for the look-a-like to fly back to The Cube in Kinji's place and quickly retire into Kinji's garden room, where she would enjoy her best acting job ever! Lounging in the presidential retreat, sipping wine and eating chocolate covered strawberries – oh how she pined to tell people! But sworn secrecy was the condition of her employment. There was hint of more work if she was trustworthy, and threats of being accused of traitorous acts if she wasn't.

The odds of a national emergency occurring during that two hour window when the presidency would be occupied by a B-movie actress were slim, but it was a frightening possibility nonetheless. Therefore, the escape plan, should the garden alarm sound, was for the look-a-like to activate an emergency signal and hide in the garden dressing room until Kinji arrived. It was a shaky plan, but one that might work if they were in a jam.

This whole nonsense is ridiculous, Ann told herself. I'm President of the United States and I'm sneaking around like a teenager climbing out a window.

Lehman and the rest of the group stood up when Ann entered the school cafeteria. They were speechless; an effect Ann was accustomed to, and bored with. Serena, seldom without something to say, was not under the Kinji spell. "As you can see, I'm not dead."

Ann hurried to give Serena a quick hug. "I'm so glad you are alive and well."

The four men silently observed the two women. Estep had an expression of horror on his face, which Serena noticed and addressed, "Don't look at me like that. I'm not the president's secret advisor, but it's nice to know that I inspire that much confidence in you."

Ann turned to face the group. "What is this motley crew I'm looking at? Paul out of prison? What's the story on that? Lehman, what kind of ragtag team did you put together? I only have a few minutes, and I have a bombshell of my own. Someone give me the condensed play-by-play."

"I'll do it," said Serena. "Special Agent Estep over here picked me up and enjoyed my sparkling conversation for the past couple of days." Estep growled, which delighted Serena. She continued, "Seriously though, he did pick me up and he told me about Covert Coffee. They worked behind-the-scenes to protect you, so I guess you could call it Covert Coffee-in-Coffee."

Ann shifted her eyes dramatically away from Serena and locked eyes with Lehman.

"Serena, I'll take it from here," he said. He

gestured toward an empty chair. Serena obediently sat, and for the second time during this operation the flush of humiliation brought warmth and color to her face.

Lehman began. "I did as you requested. Beav is one of my assembled team members, you recall he was terminated."

"Oh yes, I remember Beav," said Ann.

"These others are not my pick. Serena was already inside the lab when I arrived. Estep came at the same time I did, with Paul. He'll have to address that – I still don't know why Paul is here."

"You talk about me like I'm not in the room," said Paul.

"If you don't keep your mouth shut, you won't be in the room," said Estep.

Lehman continued, "I sent Beav to Germany to meet with your guy. It was enlightening to say the least. I have Beav's report right here." He handed Ann a document. "In a nutshell, the Social Media Channel is being controlled by several parties, some of them are our own government, some are leaders of other countries. We suspect that this is what is behind your traitorous situation in the Cube. Certain parties want to control what we see, for example, special interest groups. We have reason to believe that FYD might be one of those groups."

"What gives you reason to believe that? Is this something that came out of the Germany meeting?" asked Ann.

"No. It was something that Erik Chapman said before he died," Estep interjected.

Ann's face revealed her shock, "Erik's dead? What happened?"

"Madam President, he wasn't one of the good guys," said Beav.

"I see," Ann said quietly. "Go on."

"We can't vouch for Erik's credibility. There were some unusual circumstances," said Lehman. The five of them exchanged nervous glances. "But, we do know that he was privy to something, and we should start with FYD."

"Good work. This is certainly explosive enough to be the motivation behind the stink in the Cube. The conspiracy theorists will be happy: finally proof that the government wants to control information and brainwash them," said Ann.

"And not only our own government, but others as well," Beav reminded her.

"Yes, this is a problem bigger than the

presidency, which leads me to my bombshell. Vice President Morgan Canon has pointed the finger at someone inside the Cube who is responsible for all of this," said Ann. She paused.

Serena couldn't stand the suspense. "Who?"

"Ted."

"Your husband Ted?" asked Serena.

"Madam President, I don't believe the First Gentleman would ever betray our country," said Lehman.

"Of course not! Morgan is stalling. I assume he thinks he's established doubt in my mind and I'll waste time investigating. I don't know what his thinking was really. But clearly he is involved. What's scary is that he was so cocky. What is he doing that he thinks will all turn out in his favor if he stalls me a little? He's not stupid. He knows I'll dig until I get the truth and that won't take long," said Ann.

"You forgot about me, didn't you?" said Paul.

"Yes, what about you? Why are you here?" asked Ann.

Serena stood up from her time-out chair. "I asked for him."

17

"Please end the suspense. Why did you ask for Paul?" asked Ann.

"When I was investigating Lora, you might remember that she wrote a Town Hall message?"

"Yes, I remember, go on," said Ann. She waved her hand impatiently, a trademark Kinji gesture that had been mimicked and made popular by a talented young Asian comedienne on the new-format Saturday Night Live.

Serena wondered why Ann was so snappish.

Was it the pressure of the situation that was causing her to be so cross, or was it Serena herself who was the inspiration for the president's caustic tone? It wasn't a question she dared ask aloud. Instead, she brought herself back around to the matter at hand. "I was investigating Lora and found that her mother was in the same prison as Paul."

"The prison for the criminally insane."

"Yes. I don't know what I was fishing for, but on a hunch I got my hands on the visitors log. The records were on the system. Lora's mom got a lot of interesting visitors, but one in particular stood out. Although it's not quite the shock and awe it would have been if we didn't already know he was dirty."

"Who?"

"Erik Chapman. He visited Lora's mom in prison. I'm guessing he didn't expect anyone to ever look at the records, why would they?"

"It's odd, but what does this mean?" Ann looked reflective, as if she was puzzling it out, but in reality her mind was already multi-tasking through other items on the daily agenda. Even though her presidency had become absurdly bogged down with overlaying conspiracies, Americans still needed her to go through the motions of governing.

"I don't know, that's why I wanted to talk to Paul." Serena studied Ann's face for any sign that she approved.

"That's it? That's the only reason why Paul has been smuggled out of prison?

"Erik wasn't alone." Serena said mysteriously.

"Am I supposed to guess who was with him? Was it Morgan Canon by any chance?"

"Why yes, it was Morgan Canon, Vice President of the United States of America."

"Now that is certainly interesting enough to get Paul out of prison." Ann's tone warmed instantly. "Good work."

"I have to admit, she did get the job done," said Estep, who until now had stayed out of the conversation and far outside of Ann and Serena's personal space bubbles.

Serena studied his face but found no trace of sarcasm and no hint of a snide remark forming on his lips. "Thank you?" She dangled her question mark.

"Hey, whatever you think of me, I like you. I didn't like being assigned as your babysitter," said Estep in what was the closest thing to a peace offering Serena would receive. That, and the big smile he flashed her, a smile with the power to induce screaming and fainting in pubescent girls, a magic lost on Serena.

"The mission is exciting enough for you now I assume. Keep at it. I need to get back to the Cube before my look-alike is discovered," Ann said.

"What would you like us to do?" asked Serena.

"You aren't doing anything. You're coming with me. Ted is waiting for us on a private airstrip. Tom and the kids are with him. You do remember those people, right? Lehman, I need you—you're coming too," said Ann.

"But what about me? I didn't tell what I know yet," whined Paul.

Ann avoided any personal interaction with Paul but addressed the group as a whole. "Beav and Estep can get Paul's story and return him to prison. Tie up loose ends and report to Lehman. Anything else I need to know before I go?"

"There's something I'd like to say if I may, Madam President," said Beav.

Ann nodded.

"This is most unusual for a President to be so deeply involved in an investigation, and I admire you for it. I know you are trying to set things right.

But President Kinji, if I should be so bold, you are putting yourself in a dangerous position, and thereby putting the nation as a whole in a vulnerable state. Please go back to being President and let us do what we do," said Beav.

"I appreciate you," said Ann. "And if I'm reading between the lines correctly, what you plan to do is something I will never hear about, and should never know about." She made eye contact with Beav to confirm his understanding, and communicate her consent.

On that note, President Ann Kinji left Leesburg Elementary with Lehman; who was more than willing to be in service to the President and First Gentleman again, but was already missing his wife; and Serena, who was so impatient to see her family that she had stopped listening to anything that was said.

When the three of them were on their way, Beav and Estep flanked Paul and herded him toward the government issue sedan parked in the empty back lot. Estep drove, Beav rode shotgun, and Paul had the backseat to himself, where he sat comfortably while sharing all that he knew, or most of what he knew.

"Let me begin with an overview of my life in prison," said Paul.

Estep and Beav exchanged a look. Neither said anything, not wanting to risk Paul taking even longer to tell his story. Estep concentrated on driving while Beav kept a sharp eye out for anyone following them.

"In regular prison there are big officers with equipment and a chip on their shoulders who step in if inmates are behaving badly; like if they are beating up a fellow prisoner, medical staff, or even the guards. But in the prisons for the mentally insane, or ill -- pick your terminology of preference-- there are only petite staff members to stop the madness if they are even around to help, and that's a big if.

I'm sure you noticed this scar I got on my cheek, what a handsome tat, don't you agree? I got it because most inmates walk around free, completely unshackled. And unlike inmates in a regular prison, the mentally insane are not under threat of going 'to the hole' if they misbehave, ditto for the fear of having a prison sentence extended – that tool is not in the toolbox. Take away the punishments, there's no incentive for inmates to cooperate.

A prison for the criminally insane is a fertile ground for crime. Of course one would assume that the fertile ground for crime implies the prison populace. Enter our good friends, Mr. VP himself Morgan Canon and one of his minions Erik Chapman. Isn't Erik an uptight and unlikely name for a minion?" Paul waited for a reaction. Receiving none, he continued.

"Serena already told you that Erik was a regular visitor to see Lora's mother, Vanessa. I so adored that woman, such a temptress. She had bad luck with men, liked the bad boys, and ran wild from the tender age of twelve until shortly after she turned twenty. That's when she was ready to settle down. She gave up on the bad-boy losers and went looking for a rich older man, much older. She was tired of men wiping out her bank account, squatting in her house, and using her body like a carnival ride.

With a sugar daddy, she figured two out of three aint bad. Plus if her future husband was old enough, her body wouldn't be in demand as often, or so she thought. She liked being taken care of, thought she had found the answer for her disastrous life. She'd been a runaway, and nearly a prostitute. She really had nothing left to lose, or so she thought, so she married the first one who asked."

Estep groaned, and then snapped. "Move on!"

Paul continued, "Long story short…"

"Not short enough!" Estep snapped.

"…the old codger abused Vanessa. He belittled her, he bullied her, and he babied her. He treated her like his princess, but also his possession. And when Vanessa ended up pregnant with Lora, he kept Vanessa in one wing of his mansion – I did mention he was disgustingly rich, right?

He kept her behind lock and key until she had the baby, right there in one of the rooms in her wing. He didn't even hire a midwife for her. She had the help of the untrained housekeeping staff, and that's it. They sure got more than they bargained for that day.

Lora was born healthy and fine, no problems, but she was not a boy. Vanessa's husband had no interest in a daughter – in fact he wanted to send Lora away, while keeping Vanessa as his wife and prisoner. Well, call it temporary insanity, postpartum depression, or a mental snap brought on by years of abuse: Vanessa went nuts. She bludgeoned the nasty old bugger to death. She hid his body, stayed on at the mansion and raised Lora there as if nothing had happened.

She didn't get caught until Lora was almost four years old. No one much liked her husband, and since he was frequently out of the country, no one had inquired after him. After all, he had no real job, being independently wealthy and retired. He wasn't a philanthropist, so he never attended any fundraisers. He wasn't a big part of the social scene and he was unpopular everywhere he went anyway, so people left the situation alone.

It was only after a neighbor's dog got into the estate gardens and began digging that Vanessa's crime was discovered. He brought bones back home with him. Even then, his owners didn't catch on until he brought them the matching skull."

"I remember this story now," said Beav. "Didn't they call her The Grave Digger Widow? If she's the one, she was stunning. It was hard to believe she was a cold blooded killer – until she opened her mouth. She was a hard one."

"Yes, that would be Vanessa. But she's lost the hardness. She's so docile now, you wouldn't know she was the same girl. She's almost dotty, even without her meds. Like I said, I adored that woman."

"Why are you using past tense? Did something happen to her?" Beav's antennae were raised.

"I don't know. They came and got her one day, I never saw her again. By 'they' I mean FBI or whatever you guys are. They didn't introduce themselves and as you know, I'm America's favorite hero-slash-villain. I was a fly on the wall."

Beav turned around in his seat to look at Paul. "So far, you haven't told us anything useful. If you don't have anything productive to contribute, I vote we return you to prison before you warp our minds."

Estep snorted, a derivative of laughter; not to be confused with the contemptuous snort that he had perfected when assigned to Serena.

"I'm flattered, but my power to brainwash has dissipated." Paul looked wistfully out the window at the other drivers and passengers sharing the same stretch of road. How many of them had dinner waiting for them at home?

Estep knocked him out of his reverie. "You sound like an old guy when you talk. Prison has aged you, and made you even weirder. Seriously, you need to start saying something useful or else we're dropping your sorry deranged hide off at the boobyhatch."

"Okay then, I'll admit I do know what happened to Vanessa. They made a deal of some sort with her and arranged an early release. She's at home, sipping tea and reading chick-lit. I never could turn her on to the classics. She writes me letters every now and then."

Beav longed for a few moments of silence, but he knew he had to get this over with. "This act of yours is tiresome. You know what we want to hear."

"You can't blame me for milking my hour of attention for all it's worth. You can't imagine what it's like to have no one to talk to for hours and hours, day after day, which brings me to what I know. I spent so much time on the Social Media Channel that I picked up on patterns. Solitude can do that, you know, make one's mind sharp and focused.

I was obsessed with the SM Channel. I never turned it off. I was tracking everyone I knew on there, and then I added hundreds I didn't know, across all the platforms. I was memorizing

180

everything; user names, posts, tweets, statuses: everything that went out there. I even kept track of the global ticker tape of SM highlights. And when the data grew too large to keep in my head I put it all in a journal. Pages and pages of pointless information."

"This is pointless information," growled Estep.

"No, it's backstory. You need to know that I was in a zone, manic, scribbling in my journal. It's important because I have the journal. Not only that journal, but twenty-seven others just like it. You'll want to remember this because the journals are evidence."

"Evidence of what?" Beav was optimistic that Paul had finally started down a productive path.

"I was writing down the posts in real time, but tracking them afterward too. I don't know why, I was obsessed. It was an OCD thing, a way of coping with prison life. When people post something it scrolls off the screen a few seconds later, you get what I'm saying?"

"Yes, I know what you mean." Beav pushed the dialog forward. "And I think I know where you are going with this. People never bother to see if their posts are still there later. Are you saying they were deleted?"

"No, I'm saying they were edited."

Again Beav attempted to hurry the conversation along. "How so? Language or violent content removed? You mean censored?"

"No, worse than that. I mean that the posts were re-written. I need my journals. I could show you line by line, all easily verified if you subpoena the SM Channel."

"Think of some off the top of your head," Beav prodded. He avoided looking at Estep because the bulging vein at his temple pulsated in a most alarming manner.

"Many of the edits are to avoid bad PR, like a status that says 'I hate XYZ cars, they don't get the gas mileage they claim' would be altered to say 'I buy only XYZ cars, they live up to the gas mileage claim'."

Estep yanked the wheel, swerved across two lanes of traffic, and parked the car on the shoulder with a shriek of the brakes that reflected his mood. He glared at Paul, whose face was now ashen. "Stop jacking us around."

Paul was at a loss for words.

Beav also turned around in his seat for a stare-down with Paul. "Spammers are of trivial concern. Are you saying you have nothing more than this?"

"I'm not talking spammers. I'm talking hackers. You're not hearing me. These are posts already on SM Channel, they are no longer 'live' in real time. They have scrolled off. Then they are altered. Big corporations are involved in this fraud; it's not your kid in the basement doing this. It's big money, fraudulent business practices."

"If the messages are gone, why would this benefit the corporations at all?" Beav didn't know if he wasn't following what Paul was saying or if Paul was spinning nonsense. Either scenario was equally plausible.

"I didn't say they were gone. I said they had scrolled off. Once they scroll off they are still forever searchable. Anyone looking for an XYZ car could call up hundreds, maybe thousands of favorable posts. The negative reviews are edited to the point of non-existence."

"What is the XYZ car you are talking about?" Beav made yet another attempt to find a point to grasp hold of.

Estep burrowed his head into his folded arms on the steering wheel. He let his right arm dangle, he grunted, and then he lifted his hand to turn off the ignition. He returned his arm to the steering wheel and held that position for several minutes.

"I know that I'm getting under your skin, but you are getting under my skin as well. The XYZ car isn't important. I made up the XYZ to indicate a random generic company. This isn't even of interest to you, this is still backstory. Bear with me. Let me try this again."

Estep made a wailing sound that was muffled by his arms.

"Hackers are altering posts, obviously getting paid by major corporations to paint their products or services in a positive light, scrubbing negative reviews, all to cover up their flaws, negative perceptions, bad customer service record, or even outright wrongdoing. But, that's not your deal, I know. What I'm leading up to is that corporations aren't the only ones doing this."

"You're saying that governments are doing this?" Beav's hopes rose that Paul had finally done it; he had finally gotten to something worth saying.

"Yes, there's—"

Beav interrupted. "A crack? Look, Paul, I hate to burst your bubble, but I already know this. Some foreign dude in Germany told me. But I'm curious about what you know about it."

"A German? Not foreign if you were in Germany," said Paul, pouting.

"No, he wasn't German. Not sure what he was. But anyway, he already told me about the crack in the SM Channel, and if you were eavesdropping back at the lab, and I'm sure you were, you knew this. Is that all you've got, a regurgitation of what you overhead us saying?"

"Did your German whistle blower offer you proof?" Paul made it clear from his tone that he expected Beav's answer to be no.

"Not German, and no. Are we back to your journals again?"

"I wrote down everything. You can verify it all. You'll especially find the references to the FYD interesting, and Erik, and the VP."

"Why didn't you lead with this?" Estep untangled himself from the steering wheel and started the engine.

"You needed the backstory," said Paul.

"No we didn't!" Estep peeled away from the shoulder and nearly hit a SUV driven by someone talking on the phone while also eating a sandwich.

Beav noticed the sandwich. "I'm hungry, let's stop for some grub."

Estep jabbed a thumb toward the backseat. "We can't go inside with him. I'll pull off at the next rest stop and park by the truckers. Get me whatever, as long as you don't forget a large coffee, black."

"I'll take a Reuben if they have it," said Paul.

Both agents immediately flipped Paul off in twin-like synchronization.

The two fell into silence so dark and hunger-driven that even Paul knew better than to open his mouth. When Estep pulled into the truck stop Beav popped out of the car, walked briskly inside, ordered the food, and waited on a bench until the order was ready. Estep slept in the driver's seat while Paul stared at his hands, brooding about his lot in life.

Beav waited for over twenty minutes for the order to be ready, but he didn't mind. He knew he would only pick at this nasty stuff anyway. He sat on the bench by the truck stop door and ate the tuna he brought with him. When the order was finally ready he emerged victoriously with two large white bags laden down with hot food. The grease was soaking through the bag and so was the aroma. He set the bags inside the car, took one look at Estep's granite face and marched back into the diner to fetch a large black coffee.

After Beav re-entered the car the three ate, each man concentrating on chewing. Paul knew better than to talk. Before prison, Paul had been a slick con artist, popular with the ladies, charming, playing his good looks to his best advantage. He hated seeing himself through Estep's eyes, and Beav's as well. Paul was pathetic and annoying, scrabbling for their attention like a puppy. Well, no more. He was getting a grip on himself. He would wait until they asked for him to speak, and then he would blow them away with what he knew.

"I need to get out and stretch," said Estep.

"What were you doing all this time?" Beav couldn't imagine Estep staying in the vehicle with Paul.

"He was sleeping," Paul volunteered, already breaking his code of silence.

Estep and Beav ignored him. Estep took a short walk around the parking lot and came back to the car. He got in quickly, belted up and headed back to the freeway.

"Tell us what you know. We're taking you back. We have officially run out of time. If you really do have something to say, do it now," said Beav.

Paul launched into his story without hesitation. "Erik and the VP Morgan Canon were there at the prison and I overheard them talking about FYD. What I couldn't hear directly I either got as a recap from Vanessa, or I could decipher by reading their lips."

"Lay it on me," said Beav.

"I need something first."

"Here we go," said Estep. "I was waiting for you to start in with that. This is why you've been stalling."

"What do you want?" asked Beav.

"I want to see Serena Wilcox. We didn't have time to talk."

Estep said, "That's your one wish? You do belong in the nut house."

"What do you want to see her for?" asked Beav.

"There's something I wanted to tell her, only her."

"Well, I can't arrange that. Serena is with the

president back in Chicago, you know that. Why didn't you manage a conversation when you were with her?" Beav took over the conversation because Estep was too aggravated to speak.

"Someone was always around."

"Look, we're all you've got. Either give us your message or keep it to yourself. We are only five miles from the prison," said Beav.

Paul reflected upon that for a few seconds and then said, "Look into FYD."

"That's it? You aren't going to tell us anything else?" Beav could feel his blood pressure rising.

"Morgan wants her taken out," said Paul quietly.

"Who? Serena?" Estep was back in the conversation.

"He means President Kinji, don't you, Paul?" Beav congratulated himself at that moment for sticking with the interrogation no matter how tedious. This news was obviously way more than they thought Paul would deliver, and Beav shuddered to think what would have happened if they hadn't persevered. Would anyone have extracted this lead from Paul?

"Yes. That's what I meant. I didn't realize it

until we were in the lab and I saw Erik's, uh, disguise. The strange clown thing, and how he was going around as Victor. It struck me why he was doing it."

By this time they were at the prison, parked and hanging on to Paul's every word. He finally had their undivided attention. Too bad his big moment was shattered by the blare of half a dozen sirens surrounding their vehicle. An officer stepped out and met Estep at his now-open window.

"You're late," he said.

"Sorry, got delayed," said Estep, with no hint of apology in his voice.

"Had to pull people off their shifts for this," he said.

Beav interjected before Estep could further antagonize the officer. "He's here now. You want to take him, or should we drive on through?"

The officer waved them through, then signaled for all but his own squad car to head on out. Once the windows were back up Paul started talking, as fast as he could get the words out:

"Victor had facial recognition ID for the highest levels of security at The Cube. That's got to be what Erik was up to. That's how they are going to get the president. Listen, I know you don't trust me, but deep down I'm a good guy, right? I'm not a face-chewer. I'm not your average insane criminal. I'm more of a vigilante, wouldn't you say? I like Ann Kinji. She never saw me as trash, always respected that I had something. When she was firm with me she was only doing her job. She actually believed I could be more. Her disgust in me was because I was, I suppose, a bad seed, but she never disrespected my potential. I'm telling you the truth. I know what I know. Take my journals, you'll see. Oh, and put that genius kid Nicholas on the crack in the SM Channel. There's a private conversation between Erik and the VP that you'll want to see. It's all in my journal, the purple one, volume 5."

Parked, doors open, and their passenger unloaded, Estep and Beav watched Paul as he was escorted into the building. He turned his head to look back one last time and mouthed a word they could clearly read off his lips, "Journals".

NATALIE BUSKE THOMAS

18

Vice President Morgan Canon blinked his rodent eyes rapidly. He was an eye-blinker when he was lying. "Everything's under control," he said.

"You forget I was married to you once, Morgan. Your pants are on fire." Lita flexed her lips into an unnatural smile.

"What do you want me to say? That everything has hit the fan? You want the truth, how's this for truth: Erik's dead. He died in that stupid clown getup."

"Only a matter of time before they figure out what that's for."

"Right. We have to move fast, and get Marci out of the way. She's a loose cannon after IDing Erik at the morgue."

"She'll be back soon."

"Marci?"

"No, Madam President."

"Back? I thought she was here." Morgan couldn't hide the startled look on his face from Lita, the woman who knew his every micro-expression. For the first time, he realized that he wasn't being kept in the loop.

"No, she slipped out. She left a body-double in her place, but that fooled no one."

"Where did she go?"

"Minneapolis."

"Minneapolis? Are you sure?" Morgan frowned. "This isn't good."

"They landed somewhere near there."

"Then drove somewhere else," he said with a flat tone of conviction and defeat.

"I take it that you know where that somewhere else is?"

"I have a fair idea. The lab is up north."

"The top secret Superman lab?"

"And we can guess what they were up to."

"I'm one step ahead of you. We have eyes on their investigation. They are closing in, Morgan. You'll have to take that Toto down."

"Toto?" Morgan never did enjoy Lita's sense of humor and he was gritting his teeth through it now.

"The witch threatens to take down Dorothy…" Lita mimicked Miss Gulch's voice, "…and her little dog too." She noted Morgan's expression of non-comprehension. She added, "Kinji's the dog."

"You must be the witch," he said, playing along. Rushing Lita through these things was never a wise idea. Without a clue in his head about what was going to happen to him in the next thirty seconds he asked, "Who's Dorothy?"

"You are."

Morgan's ex-wife leveled an adorably jeweled purse-sized handgun at the face she used to wake up to every morning, with the exception of those mornings when he was with his mistress: her very own dearly departed sister Lora. Funny how she held it against Lora until Lora died. Upon her sister's death Lita's rage transferred to Morgan, and intensified ten-fold.

Morgan's mouth made an O shape, his rat-like eyes large and round for the first, and last, time in his life. Even his nose seemed to morph into one big circle like a bull's eye. Her petite gun with bling and a white pearl handle looked like it should make a cute little popping sound. It didn't. It made a single ear-shredding crack. That was all it took to blow Morgan's head off at close range. Lita's years of target practice were overkill because, in the end, she shot him from only two feet away.

No one heard the shot that ended Morgan Canon's life, as it happened at his estate in a secluded area. Lita stood over his body for a few seconds, fixing her eyes upon his lifeless face. He doesn't look much different dead than alive, she thought. Then she made the call for a cleanup crew to take care of the situation. Because, while Lita had agreed to do it, she wasn't the person who had ordered the hit. Oh no, this was not a domestic situation but a well-planned execution. She had merely wanted to be the one to pull the trigger.

19

President Ann Kinji put word out that she needed to see the VP immediately. He wasn't answering any of her attempts to reach him, something she made clear to all of her staff that she was displeased about. Not for a minute did she suspect that he had come to a bad end. She assumed that he was still alive and well, plotting evil plans to overthrow her presidency, and avoiding her.

She was partly right: someone was plotting and hatching, but certainly not the man who lay cold and rigid on the custom marble flooring now accented by blood-spatter décor that really made the whole room pop. No, Morgan Canon was out of the picture. But, with no knowledge of his death, Ann's team was still actively looking for him, and investigating everything to do with him.

Fortunately their priority was with official contacts, not personal. Had they known about Morgan's demise and Lita's involvement they would have been thrown off course. But because they had no idea what happened they were still plodding along toward answers. In this way, Lita did them a favor. Her quiet execution in Morgan's own home bought them all more time.

While Ann carried out her presidential routine as usual, allowing herself to be shuttled from one briefing to the next, Serena Wilcox was reunited with her family in The Cube's party room; enjoying karaoke, movies, snacks, and family entertainment. After a day or two of this impromptu reward vacation, Ann would send the five of them home. Serena was, after all, a private citizen.

Ann questioned her wisdom in even befriending Serena on a personal level, let alone using her as, what, a rouge agent? Was Ann so needy that she would glom on to a rather amateur former private detective for friendship? And then to go as far as to include Serena in a covert operation, one in which Ann had almost gotten her killed? She was a civilian! Did Serena even have much in the way of professional credentials? Of course her team had vetted her, but Ann hadn't even looked at the report.

No, this would be the last of their relationship. From this point on, Serena Wilcox would be one name of thousands on her automated Christmas card mailing. This being her frame of mind when Lehman appeared in her office with Serena in tow, Ann immediately stood up from her chair and stomped across the presidential seal to meet them.

"I know what you're thinking, but we need her," said Lehman.

"And why do we need her? She's a civilian. A fact I was reminding myself of right before you came in," said Ann.

"You were right to trust her, and right to maintain ties outside of The Cube. Beyond that, she's also an asset. I don't know how she does it, she's like a savant. She can get into people's heads. My suggestion? Keep her on indefinitely, bring her in when you need her as you've always done," said Lehman.

"Thank you, Agent Lehman," said Serena.

"No, no, still former agent. In fact, Madam President, if you no longer need me, I'd like to go home to my wife," said Lehman.

"Any possibility that my family can help me with the investigation?" asked Serena.

Lehman and Ann looked at her, trying to decide if she was being facetious. Seeing no guile in her face, Lehman said, "To be clear, I wouldn't recommend an official relationship with Ms. Wilcox."

"Agreed," laughed Ann. To Serena she said, "I've been standing around here giving you," she looked at the holographic clock hovering near the wall, "five minutes of the nation's time. Conspiracy or no conspiracy, leak or no leak, I have work to do."

"I'll get right to it then," said Serena. "Agent Estep and Beav checked in. They have Paul's journals, but one of them is missing – the very one he most wanted them to retrieve. Not a big obstacle, Paul says the same information is in the security crack on the SM Channel, and Nicholas can easily find it."

"Get him on it immediately," said Ann.

"No, we can't use Nicholas anymore. He's the one who got the gun in the lab. No one ever searched him – it was in his backpack," said Lehman.

"What? Not our Nicholas! I met that boy, he is an amazing young man," said Ann.

"No, he had nothing to do with it. He didn't know someone put the gun in there," said Lehman. "It had to have been one of Erik's people, whoever they may be. We are no closer on that."

"What he's trying to say is that Covert Coffee has become too dangerous for him," said Serena.

"He is a child, what was I thinking? I agree with you," said Ann.

"And that's why you can't leave, former-agent Lehman. I'm not at Nicholas' level," said Serena.

"She's right. I'm sorry, but you're needed," said Ann.

Lehman nodded. "I'm not sure I can do it either. We need Victor. But I'll see what I can do, unless you have anything else to add."

"Thank you for keeping me grounded," said Ann. "I'll get you back to your wife as soon as possible."

Lehman smiled. "Anytime." He left Serena there, but not without eye contact with Ann to confirm he should do so. Ann waved him out the door.

"Serena, Lehman's right, I need you. Both your unusual investigative help and also your friendship. Olive branch?" asked Ann.

"Of course! I didn't even realize an olive branch was needed. Consider me on the job to the end," said Serena cheerfully.

"Glad to hear it. I need to resume whatever's left of this puppet show I call a presidency," said Ann. "I leave this mess in your hands."

20

Serena met Penny in a secret tunnel of The Cube parking garage. From there, she went to a residence hall on a heavily-populated college campus. One of the residence halls was temporarily closed due to the installation of a new sprinkler system and a few other minor renovations. Between the chaos of students fetching belongings from their premises and construction workers going in and out, the dormitory was an ideal location for hiding in plain sight. They set up a makeshift conference room in one of the common areas.

Beav kicked things off. "How much time can we possibly have left? This thing should have hit the fan before now. And is President Kinji an imminent target, as in within 24 hours?"

"I don't know, but we should operate on that assumption," said Serena.

"You two might thrive on no sleep, but there isn't enough coffee in the world to keep me awake anymore," said Estep, too tired to growl. He stretched out on a well-worn and mysteriously-stained futon and within seconds was snoring at impressive decibels.

"Wow, how did he do that?" asked Serena.

"Ignore the buzz saw. Focus!" said Beav.

"Will do," Serena answered.

"I said that aloud? I was talking to myself."

The pair of them locked eyes and burst into a fit of giggles born out of sleep deprivation. Fifty-five hours without more than a few minutes of sleep here and there can do that. Serena steered them back on track. "First off, what do we know about what FYD is involved with?"

Beav launched into lecture mode, standing up and using a table as his lectern. "Biotechcrop is a big supporter of the FYD. They and others like them have been around for well over 20 years and haven't increased crop yields significantly in all that time. This lackluster result is despite an extensive effort by the industry to increase yields through GE, all of which is documented in Failure to Yield reports. Thousands of experimental field trials were carried out, involving GE – genetically engineered crops."

"Yes, I'm familiar with what GE means," said Serena.

"In all that time, and after so many experimental trials, only corn has increased yield. One likely reason is that new yield genes cause more genetic side-effects that often lead to undesirable agricultural properties. Irregardless—"

"Regardless."

"Regardless, even though GE crops haven't significantly increased yields, many farmers adopted them for protection against insect pests and other reasons."

Beav helped himself to the wall-mounted dry erase board labeled "Campus Events" and made notes as he spoke. "Prior to the introduction of HT soybeans, conventional farmers often used three or four different herbicides applied several times a year. With HT soybeans, farmers could apply glyphosate herbicide only once or twice, instead of the several applications of before, plus they could apply directly onto the crop during the growing season."

"Your agricultural lesson is relevant because?" asked Serena.

"Because it didn't work. Weeds developed resistance to glyphosate: Several million acres of GE soybeans, and even cotton, are now infested with glyphosate-resistant and tolerant weeds. The number of glyphosate applications by farmers has risen considerably, and the amount of herbicide used on HT soybeans is considerably higher than it was prior to the introduction of this HT crop."

"Ah, gotta love food technology."

"Well, I wouldn't wave it away that easily. Food technology is not a new science; we can date it way back to 1810 with the canning process. And of course there was pasteurization and I could go on with a history lesson, but you get the idea. If we were only talking about food technology flops, there would be no conspiracy theory."

"The conspiracy lies with the money, like

always."

"On the nose."

"So your theory is that the FYD stands to gain from GE technology so they are pushing it through even though it doesn't yield results, and are tampering with public reaction on the SM Channel chatter?"

"No, at least I don't think so. GE is an issue I tossed at you for an example of the type of issue FYD could possibly be protecting."

"Don't tell me you went through that whole lecture on GE foods only to tell me it's nothing more than an example!"

Beav averted his eyes sheepishly.

"You did! But why? You know we are short on time! The President could really be in danger. Unbelievable!" Serena said.

"We have to start somewhere. I think we should be looking for something like this, an issue that FYD wants to bury. And why not start with GE foods? Biotechcrop is one of FYD's biggest bankrollers. It makes sense to start with them and research what they do, which is GE foods."

Beav's lecture notes were sprawled all over the previously blank campus event board. Serena glanced over them dismissively. "You do that. Meanwhile, I'll call Lehman and see if he's arrived at the lab yet."

"No, he'll call when he has something. Let's get back to brainstorming. When he does call, something we say now could speed up the process later."

"OK then, I can think of another issue off the top of my head, one that actually turned up in our investigation. What about regulating private farms and home gardens?"

"As much as I agree it's a hot button issue, where's the big money interest in that?" Beav erased some of his notes, leaving the most important phrases behind.

Serena removed an obsolete tablet from her bag: it could still connect to the Internet in buildings that used old school connections. Campuses were notorious for lagging behind in technology, due to the cost to update entire buildings when budgets were already taxed. Her hunch was correct. Serena connected to the web without any difficulty.

"Big money? Well, like you mentioned with GE, farm regulation is not a new issue. In 1942 a

NATALIE BUSKE THOMAS

United States Supreme Court decision, Wickard v. Filburn, recognized the power of the federal government to regulate economic activity. I can read straight from Wikipedia as well as the next person. In fact, I'll do that now:

'A farmer, Roscoe Filburn, was growing wheat for on-farm consumption. The U.S. government had established limits on wheat production based on acreage owned by a farmer, in order to drive up wheat prices during the Great Depression, and Filburn was growing more than the limits permitted. Filburn was ordered to destroy his crops and pay a fine, even though he was producing the excess wheat for his own use and had no intention of selling it.'

The Supreme Court decided that 'Filburn's wheat growing activities reduced the amount of wheat he would buy for chicken feed on the open market, and because wheat was traded nationally, Filburn's production of more wheat than he was allotted was affecting interstate commerce. Thus, Filburn's production could be regulated by the federal government.'

If we bring this issue forward to more recent years, regulation included raiding family farms and

208

even threatening moms with jail time if they didn't stop distributing food to their neighbors. President Kinji made a lot of government agencies unhappy with her reversal of many of the regulations imposed upon private farms by the past two administrations," said Serena, playing professor as smoothly as Beav had.

"I'm still not seeing the big money. With GE foods, I can see major government contracts ripped out from under fat cats. Motive. Where's the fat cat in your issue?"

"I don't know, but my gut feeling is that we are looking at regulations of farms. The Town Hall messages I sifted through contained several e-mails about that issue, and I got a vibe that something was off."

"Off how?"

"The tone of the e-mail seemed inconsistent, like reading from a script. Well, technically writing from a script, which doesn't make sense. Copying from a script."

"I get it."

"I have a sixth sense for these things, it's how I roll," said Serena.

"You won't get an argument from me. I've

never been a conventional person myself. I'm going to give equal weight to both of our theories, but let's keep it between us how you came to your contribution."

"Agreed. So we brainstorm some more?" Serena added the word "farms" and a "?" to the board. "Another thought comes to mind: what about the bioterrorism threat assessments? How do those relate to the FYD? Any fat cats threatened by the president's new bill?"

"Not that I can see."

"We really need something more to go on. We're sitting around guessing and spinning theories, based on stale intel and my gut. Where's Lehman with something new?" asked Serena.

As if on cue the incoming call light finally flickered. "I have something," said Lehman. He was on conference call with the pair of them.

"We're listening," said Serena.

"It's odd. Seems the FYD wants to cover up some experimental farming with genetically engineered foods that was secretly conducted on private family farms."

In unison, and barely above a whisper, Serena and Beav said, "We were both right."

"What?" said Lehman.

"Never mind. Has the real Victor been located yet?" asked Beav.

"No, but we're closing in on him," said Lehman. "I expect they'll have him any minute now."

"A big question is, will the real Victor confirm that FYD is involved at all? Erik is the one who told us about FYD. For all we know, it was all a lie to throw us off Erik and the VP's actual game plan," said Serena.

"No, there's no doubt. We were able to confirm FYD's involvement independently of Erik. Remember we have Victor's computers, and there was a lot we could learn without cracking anything."

"How do we know that this is Victor's data?" asked Serena.

"We don't know for sure, but we confirmed they are his machines, and the data bears out what Erik told us," said Lehman.

"Why did Erik tell us all of that though? It doesn't make sense," Serena said. "Why would he confess everything? Did he expect we would believe he was the real Victor even after strip-

211

searching him at the prison door?"

"We did have his back against the wall. That's when most criminals start giving out information," said Beav.

"Besides, he told us only what we could easily learn for ourselves from Victor's computers," said Lehman.

"Next question: why was Erik at Victor's? To destroy the computers? Or was he looking for something?" asked Serena.

"I assume he was there to wipe the computers clean, but I have serious doubts he could do that. Victor would have had a back-up to the back-up, with encryptions I probably can't crack," said Lehman.

Beav said, "Whatever he was doing, he was already suited up, so to speak, for the security identification as Victor. He was off to The Cube next."

"One thing I'm not clear on- if the Victor mask looks nothing like him, how does it get him through security?" Serena had been wondering about this for a while.

Lehman gave her a simplified explanation. "Erik only needed a few points of recognition to fool the scanner. The rest of the mask could look like anything he wanted. Why he chose something so hideous, that I can't answer."

"And why was he going to The Cube?" asked Serena.

"I don't think you'll find those answers in a computer," said Beav.

"I say we talk to the vice president," said Serena.

21

Ted found it easy to bail on his self-imposed duties as First Gentleman. After all, no one expected much from him. Today's agenda had an entire two-hour block dedicated to "fitness", which usually meant a light cardio workout, a jog inside The Cube's beautifully maintained park, cool-down stretches and a visit to the sauna and shower. Secret service lagged behind, giving him the privacy he requested.

He knew that when he didn't take a second lap

around the park they would go looking for him, but he had plenty of time to slip away from the Cube and into a car that was waiting for him. The car, which was in most instances a government issue sedan, blended into the backdrop. The driver was again Penny, now the chauffeur of choice for all discrete travel, even road trips that President Kinji knew nothing about.

Penny drove directly to a cute suburban home in Arlington Heights, owned by Lora's grandmother. This was where Lora's mother Vanessa was currently living. She was expecting Ted. Penny waited in the car while Ted went inside. In his absence, Penny made a few calls to cover for his sudden disappearance. She blamed his absence, and her pick-up, on a sudden-onset gastrointestinal issue. She assured his detail that everything was under control. She did all of this partly out of patriotic duty (not to mention the generous off-the-books paycheck) and partly out of guilt.

After all, she was the one who had first alerted President Ann to the situation. If anything went wrong, she would always second guess her decision to come forward. If not for her, maybe this mess would have been the next administration's nightmare; dear Ann could have quietly retired into a much deserved uneventful life at the end of her presidency. Penny was going to do whatever she could to help, even if it meant lying to the president.

While Penny waited and kept a watchful eye out for any suspicious activity, Ted meanwhile was greeted, seated, and left alone with Vanessa. He cleared his throat, which prompted her to ask him if he wanted a glass of water. He declined.

"Mr. President's Husband, what do you want with me?" asked Vanessa. "Is President Ann as pretty in person as she is on TV?"

Ted decided to ignore the question; he had no time for fluffy conversation. "I need to know about your arrangement with FYD."

"My what? Honey, I have no idea what you are talking about. Are you sure you're talking to the right person?"

"You had visitors when you were in prison from the vice president and Erik Chapman."

"Oh, that's what all this is about! Sure, they came many times, but they weren't there to talk to me."

"No? The log shows that they were there to see you."

"Yes, I know. They saw me, but they said it was the only way to see Victor – that's who they really came to see, not me."

"Why didn't they see Victor directly?"

Vanessa looked surprised. "Oh, oops, I bet I wasn't supposed to talk to you. I thought you were in on it too."

"In on what? You might as well tell me the rest. I can find it out for myself."

Vanessa seemed to think it over for a few seconds, but she was eager to spill what she knew. "They didn't want anyone to know that they were interested in Victor, so they asked me to keep quiet."

"Do you know what they wanted with him?" Ted examined her face to judge her reaction.

"No." Vanessa's eyes slid down and to the left.

Ted had had enough psychology classes to know that this was a classic sign that Vanessa was lying. "The truth now please? It could help the president."

Vanessa fidgeted with the bangle on her wrist. "They did ask me to pass messages back and forth."

"Do you know what these messages were about?" Ted's focus on her face was unwavering.

NATALIE BUSKE THOMAS

Vanessa blushed. "I may have looked at them."

Ted softened his tone. "You aren't in any sort of trouble. Please tell me what the messages said." His soothing voice, his refined good looks, his caring eyes – he used them all to give her his charming best.

Vanessa met his eyes and nearly swooned. "I can do better than that. I copied them."

"You did? How did you manage that?" He exaggerated, by using a dramatic tone and even more dramatic facial expression, how impressed he was. He downplayed his eagerness to see those pages. He would keep this all about her, and flatter her as much as he could.

"I wrote them down, word for word. I have a friend in there. He keeps journals of everything important. He loaned me one of his journals." Vanessa touched her hair and began twirling it around her finger.

"This friend, would he be Paul Tracy by any chance?" Ted moved a little closer to her.

"Yes! How did you know that?" Vanessa batted her false eyelashes and leaned in closer to the handsome First Gentleman in the pin-striped shirt. She was so close that she could smell his cologne.

Idly she wondered if President Ann had bought it for him.

"It doesn't matter. We already have his journals, but there is one missing." Ted stared meaningfully at her face. He had a hunch...

"That's because I have it. He told me to keep it in a safe place, and that one day someone would come looking for it." Vanessa looked pleased with herself. She knew that she had supplied the answer that Ted was hoping for.

"That day is today. I'm the someone who is looking for it."

"I'm not sure yet." Vanessa fidgeted with her bangle again, this time dropping it on the floor. She picked it up and slid it back onto her wrist.

"Not sure you should trust me?" Ted gestured at himself with both hands and tried to make light of her reservations, but his playfulness only intensified her bangle twisting.

"Paul said not to give the journal to anyone who doesn't know the answer to a question."

"What is the question?" Ted imagined a bangle on his own wrist; it was his turn to feel anxious. He hadn't known there would be a riddle involved.

"It doesn't make any sense."

"Try me."

"Who is Victor?"

"What do you mean? You know who Victor is." Ted realized he had lost control over the conversation, and no amount of posturing was going to bring it back around in his favor.

"No, that's the question Paul gave me. 'Who is Victor?'"

Ted took a stab at it. "Victor is Erik?"

"No," said Vanessa, shaking her head woefully. "That's not it. I can't help you."

"Wait! I think I know. The answer is 'a clown'." Ted slapped his fist into his hand. That had to be it, he got it!

Vanessa stood up. "Yes! That's the right answer! You are that someone. I'll get it for you." She left the room for a few minutes. Ted could hear the sounds of her rummaging through drawers. As the minutes began to drag on, he worried that she couldn't find the journal, but she eventually emerged with a triumphant smile on her face. "I found it! It wasn't where I left it, I swear." She handed the journal to Ted.

Ted thumbed through it and frowned. "There are pages torn out of this one too."

"Really? It wasn't like that when Paul gave it to me."

"Are you looking for these?" A woman's voice came from behind them.

The hairs on the back of Ted's neck stood up. He knew who it was before turning around. "Marci? What are you doing here?"

Marci stood with her legs spread apart; a firmly rooted tree, her arms branches over her head. She rustled the torn pages like they were her leaves. Her face was stretched as if she had her hair pulled back too tightly. Her mouth was twisted. Her eyes were dilated.

"I'm sorry about your husband," said Ted. He took a few steps toward Marci while Vanessa froze.

"Don't come any closer! Erik told me all about you, and your grab for power. You are the one behind all of this. You are the one who hired my husband. You killed him!"

Ted showed the palms of his hands. "I'm not going to hurt you, clam down and let's discuss this."

"No, no! You stay right there!" Marci let the pages flitter to the floor as she scrabbled at the buttons of her oversized denim shirt to reveal a bra

221

stuffed with something awkwardly bulky; an object Vanessa instantly recognized.

"Lora's gun! Where did you get that?"

A look of bewilderment passed over Marci's face, as if Vanessa's voice had confused her. She rebounded quickly and said, "I forgot you were Lita's mother."

"Lita wouldn't have given you her sister's gun, I know she wouldn't," said Vanessa.

"Of course she would, she did. A mother's love is always blind. Lita had her own axe to grind. Do you think she'd let Lora's memory go un-avenged?"

Vanessa gasped. "What did she do? Where is she?"

Marci removed the petite bejeweled gun from her bra and leveled it at Ted. "I don't know where Lita is. I have my own issue to deal with."

Ted adopted a soothing tone. "Marci, put the gun down. I'll do whatever you want. Just please, let's talk."

"What did Lita do? I have to know," Vanessa pleaded.

Ted walked a step closer to where Marci was standing.

"Don't move!" Marci shrieked. The gun wavered precariously at the end of her outstretched arm.

Ted let his arms fall passively until his fingertips rested upon his outer thighs. He stood without wavering, taking deep and controlled breaths. He waited.

Vanessa took her cue from Ted. She too struck a non-threatening pose and stood silently motionless. The minutes ticked by and it felt as if they had spent hours holding steady, casting their eyes submissively on the floor, trying not to think about the gun that Marci was holding in her trembling hand.

"Erik told me everything," Marci repeated. Her voice was flat now, her eyes dull and lifeless. "I know about your affair with Morgan's wife."

Vanessa forgot her code of silence and the threat of being shot. Her addiction to gossip overtook her. "The Vice President's wife? Oh poor President Ann!"

"Yes, can you believe it? They were together the entire time Kinji's been President, even before. Ted's no gentleman. He wants his wife out, himself in." Marci frowned. "But he couldn't do it without my Erik's help. And now Erik is dead." She held the light-weight gun with both hands to steady her aim.

"What is it that you want from me?" asked Ted.

"I want you dead!" Marci screeched.

"I can help you find the person who killed your husband." Ted made another attempt to move closer, his arms remaining limp at his sides, his gait slow.

"You killed him!" Marci was now racked with sobs, the gun shakier than ever.

"No, it wasn't me. You are right, I was pushing for the presidency. With the FDA lobbyists, and others, in my pocket, I could easily win an election."

"Where you planning to take the VP's wife too?" Vanessa's voice dripped with contempt, making it clear with one tone change that she had switched teams.

"No. She and Morgan were finished anyway, but no, we weren't staying together. She was a passing amusement," said Ted with nonchalance.

"A passing amusement!" Vanessa mocked.

"It was mutual. We were together for

convenience, neither of us happy. She knew about Erik and Morgan working behind the scenes to get me lined up for my run at the office. In fact, I promised Erik to tap him for the cabinet position of his choice. Morgan would be my VP of course. He knew about his wife, didn't care."

"Erik didn't tell me any of that."

"He wouldn't have told you anything important." Ted shuffled a few inches closer to the ever-shaking bejeweled gun.

"He told me everything!" Marci blinked away her tears and visibly morphed from grief back to anger.

"I highly doubt that."

"Then how do I know so much?" She relaxed her stance for a few seconds, the gun no longer locked on Ted's face. "The lobbyists have taken over the SM Channel, for one."

"Everyone knows about the power of the lobbyists. Take the food industry: Retailers, junk food manufacturers and the big Ag lobby are the USDA's customers. Nothing new there." Ted scooted his feet forward a few more inches, doing his best to keep his upper body seemingly unmoving. He kept talking. "We make no effort to

NATALIE BUSKE THOMAS

track the money spent on food stamps. Where is the
money going? Food lobbyists are going to do
whatever they can to keep their power. Like I said,
nothing new. You wouldn't need Erik to draw that
conclusion. See? He didn't confide in you."

"Yes he did! He told me about the SM Channel
secret mind control project. And I know it's not
common knowledge because it's classified at the
top levels of clearance, only scientists and top level
brass know about it." Marci looked from Ted to
Vanessa, who took eye contact as permission to
speak.

"Is that what they wanted Victor for?" asked
Vanessa. "Victor, Paul and I were friends. I saw
him leave with the VP plenty of times and I know
he was a scientist before he went crazy and killed
all those people."

"Yes, that's right!" Marci nodded at the person
she perceived as her new alliance. "They took him
to make molds of his face. Victor had the security
clearance they needed. No one had bothered to
scrub it from the system when he left, so all they
needed to do was use his identity."

"Erik came into The Cube as himself, put the
latex mask on, and then sailed right through the

areas beyond his security clearance," Ted added.

"See? You didn't think I knew all that, did you?" Marci narrowed her eyes smugly at Ted.

"What else did Erik tell you?" asked Ted.

"I proved he told me everything. I'm done talking." The finality in Marci's voice was unmistakable. She raised the gun, held it with both hands, and locked her arms out in front of her.

What happened next was a blur: Vanessa ducked behind the couch. Ted darted toward Marci. Serena, without anyone's knowledge, had entered the home from the back door that she had conveniently found unlocked. Unlike Goldilocks, she didn't find an empty house with bowls full of hot soup; she found a crazed woman holding a gun on the first gentleman. Having had learned her lesson from the incident with Eric-as-Victor, Serena didn't hesitate. She crouched down and ran, remaining hunched-over, to a position behind Marci. She hid herself by sitting down. What she did next shocked everyone, including Serena.

Aikido is a Japanese martial art designed to defend oneself while also protecting the attacker from injury. Unfortunately Serena's training was severely lacking. She had seen a demonstration of the "four-direction throw", shihōnage, in the situation of a standing attacker and seated defender, but she had never actually attempted it. The receiver of the throw should take a break-fall to safely reach the ground. Serena scooted into the proper position to perform this grappling maneuver from her seated position. At this same instant, Marci caught Serena's motion in her peripheral vision.

Serena grabbed Marci's arm to perform the throw. Marci sailed through the air – and simultaneously pulled the trigger. She landed on the floor with a hideous thud after hitting her head on the coffee table as she went down. The bullet zinged up and to the left, sailing through the drywall and lodging itself into the wall of the next room. The forensic team would find it easily when processing the crime scene later.

The clean-up crew heard the pop when Marci fired her weapon but they waited for orders before going in. The sudden appearance of squad cars and secret service agents was a game-changer. The crew drove away, wondering what went wrong in there and anxious about their vulnerability. Each man considered leaving the country before it all came down.

22

Ann listened to the entire recording. Then she said, "Do you think she went for it?"

"I certainly hope so," said Ted. "She'll talk to someone, especially if we let it happen. We might learn something."

"Why did she think you were having an affair with Morgan's wife?" asked Ann.

"I don't know. I can't figure out the logic behind that. I went with it, but wow was I nervous. I thought I would blab something that went against the story and she would know I was making things up," said Ted.

"I think I know why she thought you were having an affair. When you sneaked out of the McDonald's parking lot, did you happen to use Mrs. Canon's driver? Or her car?" asked Serena.

"You know about this?" asked Ted.

"Sir, everyone knows about this," said Beav.

"Ted, you didn't pull it off, it was on the SM Channel within the hour," laughed Ann. "And yes, he did use one of the cars assigned to her detail. You're right, I'm sure they put two and two together and came up with a scandal."

"It was in the tabloids," said Beav.

"Ah, well, I don't read those," said Ann.

"Anyway, that's not much of a mystery. But if Erik told her that you were after the presidency, he was deliberately misleading Marci. Did Marci think she was on the good side of this? And if so, why? What was Erik really up to, that he didn't want his wife to know about?" asked Serena.

"Again, nothing new. We know that they were involved in something, but Erik is dead and Morgan is missing. I'm not sure either is a threat anymore, so if this doesn't go any further we might be looking at a cold case," said Beav.

"It would be easier if we could talk to Marci," said Serena.

"What are you talking about? She's in custody, isn't she?" asked Ann.

"She might not be able to talk for a while," said Ted.

"Why not? What happened?" asked Ann. A round of snickers, coughs and snorts made it difficult for Ann to hear Serena's accounting for how Marci became incapacitated.

"I performed Aikido on her and she had an accident," said Serena.

"You performed? Like a demonstration?" Ann's eyes registered disbelief. Laughter broke out.

"No, she flipped her like a ninja," said Beav, with a note of pride.

"Serena did this? When did you learn martial arts?" Ann struggled to keep a straight face.

"I've been at it a while. First time I've ever used it in a real life situation." Serena's earlier attempt at remorse was nullified by the gloating she was doing now.

"What accident?" asked Ann.

"I flipped her and she pitched into the table.

She's concussed and in the hospital. I didn't mean to do that part, but at least she wasn't able to shoot anybody," said Serena.

"Madam President, we have people on guard at the hospital. Marci Chapman won't be an issue," said Estep.

"What was Ted doing in all of this in the first place? Why was he involved?" asked Ann.

"Sorry, he was the only person I could think of who could do some digging as a Cube insider. We had no idea Marci was there. The plan was to find out what Vanessa knew. The result was way better than expected." Serena noticed the expression on Ann's face. "Well, except for the First Gentleman almost getting killed."

"And thanks to you, I'm fine," said Ted.

"You were incredibly impressive. I can't believe how well you could improv," said Serena.

"I can't believe what you did," said Ted. "What are you, all of five two?"

"Ah, the mutual admiration club, may I join?" Ann smiled. "I would have loved to have seen Serena in action."

"Oh you can! We had video surveillance. Estep and I have watched it more than a dozen

233

times on the way over," said Beav.

"Indulge me. Package it, put a bow on it, and make it my next Christmas present." Ann quickly switched gears. While she enjoyed casual and light-hearted human moments, she was always aware that she was the President, although the title held little meaning at the moment, given that her cabinet, her staff, and even the vice president couldn't be trusted; world leaders of other nations were potential enemies, more so than usual that is, and worst of all, she was operating with a ragtag team of former agents and Serena Wilcox, who was in a class of her own. Nonetheless, she was still the acting president and she would fight to maintain some level of leadership.

She said, "While the rest of you wait for Lehman to report in with an update I need to get on with today's agenda. You'll have to excuse me while I peruse the latest Town Hall messages." Then she positioned herself in front of the screen on the back wall and turned her attention to what was on it. Everyone knew better than to join her; everyone except for Serena, who immediately stood up and walked to where Ann was already engaged in reading her inbox.

"I should read these with you," Serena said.

Ann nodded.

The two women read through the Town Hall messages while the rest of the group sat at the conference table silently waiting for Lehman to give them an update. While all were itching to get to work, they were also running on empty. Beav nodded off a few times, his arms folded upon the table as a pillow for his weary head. The minutes dragged with no activity except for the calls for Ann Kinji, all of which were routine. The President was not scheduled to be anywhere for another hour yet.

Lehman was in another wing of The Cube scouring video footage. He put everyone who was a new hire, no more than three weeks at The Cube, on alert to find what he was looking for: the image of a repulsive clown-like form of Erik-as-Victor entering and exiting the eighth floor on multiple occasions. He drafted every intern into the project, even though none of the newbies had clearances for a job that secure. They couldn't trust anyone who was working at The Cube when the first inklings of a rat started to surface. He also avoided using anyone who had connections or was over the age of twenty-two, but even with such narrow criteria to select from, he had fourteen pairs of eyes on the video feed.

Despite the unnaturally calm demeanor of President Kinji and her Covert Coffee team, time was of the essence. Ann and Serena wrapped up the Town Hall readings, finding nothing unusual. They (Beav, Estep, Penny, Serena, Ted and Ann) waited together without much conversation until Lehman reported in.

The six of them sat at a ridiculously long half-million dollar conferencing table in luxurious leather chairs. The digs weren't as exciting as the Superman lab, and the overstatement was vulgar, but the team was nonetheless relieved to be in the final stretch of the mission and sitting here instead of there. Sleep deprivation was still mostly unresolved, none of them had more than a few winks here and there when they could catch them. The offer of coffee was met with great enthusiasm by everyone but caffeine-avoider Beav.

"Finally a good cup of coffee! Covert Coffee made me crave coffee this whole time," said Serena.

There they sat, sipping coffee from red and

green mugs, sugar and cream in most of them, reflecting upon the mission's journey. A good five minutes of quiet passed, a passage of time that felt long to a crew struggling to hold on to adrenaline while waiting for answers. They ran through the events of the past 48 hours.

"With Morgan's body discovered, and Erik's body already in the morgue, the bad guys are no longer a threat, wouldn't you say? We know where the leak was," said Estep. "No disrespect, Madam President, but I question why am I still needed, why any of us are still needed. At this point, the feds and locals can take care of it."

Beav agreed, "Marci was a loose end, but she is incapacitated thanks to Betty Boop over there, and besides that she was operating out of personal motivation, not conspiracy. Domestic situation of sorts."

"This is the part when the meddling kids explain who did it and why," said Ann.

"Scooby-Doo?" Serena guessed.

"Yes, it's been a running theme in my head all day. And that's how ridiculous all of this is. You're right, Agent Estep. This has gone on long enough. I'm down to only forty-five minutes before the

GOB initiative," said Ann.

"Are we sure that Global Oil isn't involved in any of this?" asked Serena.

"We aren't sure of anything, but I need to carry on the business of the nation. You have five minutes more of my time, and then I'm off. In fact, Agent Estep, you can head on out now. I'd like you on my security detail today," said Ann.

Agent Estep needed no second invitation. He sprang out of his chair, gave them a two-fingered salute goodbye and bolted out the door before the president could change her mind.

After Estep had left the room Beav resumed dialog. "Madam President, I don't think you should stop turning over stones. The crack in the SM Channel isn't going to disappear simply because no one is fighting to keep it a secret. The mind control project is troubling as well."

"I'll keep you on until the end of the week, but after that I'll be reassigning Covert Coffee to agents who are still active," said Ann.

"The President is still in danger," said Serena.

"Is this fact or one of your hunches?" asked Ann.

Serena pointed at the door. "Fact."

Two masked figures entered the room. But it was the sight of the unmasked man between them that put fear into everyone's heart. Because, the man standing between them was Agent Lehman; bound, gagged, and strapped with explosives.

23

Before any of them could process what was happening, Agent Estep burst through the entryway. He had a dozen agents with him. At this point a chorus of "No, no, wait, wait!" and "It's a bomb!" went up, but the alarm was only coming from four of them: President Kinji, Ted, Serena and Penny. Everyone else was quiet.

When the four caught on that Estep and his team were not backing down, and furthermore, Beav was on his feet gloating, they too fell silent.

One of the masked figures, a woman, said, "What are you doing here? I thought you were fired."

Beav smiled. "Just helping out."

The figure swore, repeatedly.

"I'm confused. Why are we not worried about the bomb, is it fake?" asked Ann.

"No, it's very much real," said Beav. "But we aren't worried because it's one of mine."

"I'm in good hands," said Lehman. "He'll have this thing disarmed in seconds. You might not be aware that Beav is somewhat of a legend."

Estep jerked his head toward the two figures. His team cuffed them and dragged them out of the way. Beav ran to Lehman, grabbed the end of a small plastic strip located on the outer casing of the bomb and pulled, exposing a panel with ten digits on it. He punched in a code. The bomb beeped twice and powered down, lights out. "Voila! You're a free man, Lehman!"

"Well done, Beav!" said Ann.

Beav was speechless as he basked in his moment of personal redemption, making up for missing Paul Tracy's bomb. And wasn't President Ann the one most worth saving-- that is, if it were up to him? He stood looking at her; grinning, his eyes misting over.

Serena ended the moment. "This is the part when the gang takes the masks off the bad guys to reveal who they really are."

"Should we place bets?" asked Beav.

"You think you know who they are?" asked Ted.

"Nope, no clue," said Beav. "Serena?"

"If I had to guess, I'd say that this one is the real Victor and this one, being obviously female, is probably Lita," she said.

Estep gave President Kinji a quizzical look. Ann nodded. He signaled for his agents to remove the masks, revealing Victor and Lita, both of them red in the face from being overheated by wearing the masks.

Ann said, "How did you do that?"

"Well, you might remember that Vanessa kept asking what her daughter did, and where she was. Marci alluded to Lita having something to avenge. I figured Lita was floating out there somewhere, somehow involved in whatever was going to go down, and I'm also suspecting that she killed Morgan, by the way. When one of them was female, I thought, 'oh Lita's turned up'. As for

Victor, why hadn't anyone found him? He must have been trying to stay hidden. With our only other leads dead, he had to be Victor. Unless there was a surprise unknown candidate, which I thought was probably unlikely, so yeah, my money was on Victor. How much did I win?" Serena held her palm out.

"Does your bloodhound sense also point to where we can find evidence that will connect these two to more than what we saw for ourselves? Of course they'll never see the light of day after bringing a bomb into my office, but I want all the other rodents in the nest," said Ann.

"Yes, actually, I do know where to look. We have to get into the crack in the SM Channel. I also want those torn pages that Marci was throwing around. If I can get Paul to talk to me we might be able to get the information even faster. He obviously knows what's in those pages and for whatever reason didn't tell us," said Serena.

Lehman jumped in, "We've been working on two of those three things and are close. I'm not helping with Paul. We can do this without his help."

Serena turned to face Lita, who was standing directly behind her. "You have to know that there is absolutely no hope of you escaping prison. You might as well help us."

Lita's rage hit her with such intensity that she temporarily possessed supernatural strength. She bulldozed her way past the two agents who had been loosely restraining her. Not at all hampered by her hands cuffed behind her back, she bent her head down and charged at Serena like a bull.

Serena didn't need to remember her Aikido training; she simply had to move out of the way. Serena sprang backward with the speed and agility of a dancer. Without Serena's body to stop her, Lita was thrown off balance, sending her flying into the conference table. Her head slammed onto the tabletop and skidding into a landing just in front of Serena's green coffee cup, coffee that was now cold and completely unappetizing for other reasons. Lita's long hair spiraled across the table, blood flowing over and through it, pooling up around the coffee mug.

"She's done it again!" said Beav.

"Sorry, she won't be helpful to us now," said Serena.

"She wasn't going to tell you anything anyway," said Estep. He signaled for all of them to follow him into the blood-free adjoining room. Then he doubled-back to the scene of the newest drama. He made arrangements for three separate teams to come in and do their jobs; one of those jobs was to transport Lita to the Cube's ER wing via stretcher. Estep re-joined the others and caught up with a conversation already in progress.

"I'm going to be late for the GOB initiative if I don't leave right now," said Ann.

"I don't feel comfortable with you going. Give up on it and address the nation right now with the news of the vice president's passing. Explain that his sudden death requires your complete attention and sympathy. Back out now," said Ted.

"I agree. The plan to hold back on the news doesn't make sense anymore. Now we have these two and can piece the rest together with a little more digging. You won't be safe until we know the rest of the story," said Serena.

"I can postpone it until tomorrow, but no later. In the event of an emergency, tomorrow is the 'rain date'. I won't be consumed with the Morgan Canon situation enough to justify canceling the initiative altogether. Too many nations are involved – this has been in the works for two years," said Ann.

"Tomorrow's good. We can do that," said Lehman.

"I have a press conference to give," said Ann. "I'm leaving you to clean up this mess."

Serena said, "President Kinji?"

Ann raised her eyebrows.

"Don't say anything about what happened just now with Victor and Lita."

Ann nodded. Then she left with Penny and Ted in tow. Estep's team removed both Victor and the unconscious Lita from the room. Lehman, Estep, Beav and Serena were all that remained.

They all looked at the bloodied conference table. An investigation team would be in shortly to bag and tag, while keeping the investigation quiet of course. The sleuthing quartet needed a new room to work in; better yet, a lab fit for a super hero, complete with a young genius named Nicholas.

"How long would it take us to get back to Hudson?" asked Serena.

"You read my mind," said Lehman.

"I won't let anything happen to the kid," said Estep.

24

"It's good to be back," said Nicholas. "I'm sorry about the gun."

"That wasn't your fault," said Serena.

Lehman arranged for Nicholas' computer to be displayed on multiple monitors, including a large screen that Serena and Beav would be viewing from their location at the table. Lehman would be working alongside Nicholas. Their first order of business was to follow Victor's labyrinth until they found the crack in the SM Channel.

It wasn't difficult for either of them when they worked together. Lehman contributed what he and his team had put in and Nicholas had already stumbled on the crack by accident on a few occasions. He had used his own version of it when he connected with Paul in prison. The only real issue was finding the specific trail that Victor used so that they could retrieve his history.

Travel time shot up the rest of the work day; it was already past dinner hour and they were hungry. The good news was that the actual work to find Victor's trail took only fifteen minutes after their arrival at the lab. They sent Estep out for food while they dug into the secrets of the crack in the SM Channel. Who was talking there? And why?

The reading was juicy. They found all manner of illegal dealings and backdoor conversations. What was hilarious to them was that the conversations were treated the same as any data, and were searchable! Within seconds they found the exact conversation Paul had told them about, simply by typing in Erik Chapman and Morgan Canon. It was an audio file.

"I don't like using the Channel for this," said Morgan.

"It's safer than the phones. No tracing," said Erik.

"Victor can see it," Morgan sounded more irritated than alarmed.

"He's not looking."

"What?"

"I got him involved in a project that will keep him busy for a long time." Erik sounded smug.

"I'll be happier when he's out of the picture entirely."

"I have everything I need except for who's paying him."

Morgan was quiet for a few seconds. "Look, this has gotten out of hand. I want out."

"Too late now, you're all in."

"What are you saying?" At this point Morgan did sound alarmed.

"I have the ID. I am going through with it. You know about the plan. What do you think they will do to you if they find out you knew?"

"And how would they know if you don't tell them?"

"You're telling them right now. The crack has ears." Erik laughed. The audio file ended.

"We know why Morgan was murdered!" Beav

said.

"But we're no closer to who killed him, besides Lita being the one who did the actual deed, which forensics will prove soon," said Serena.

"Victor turned out to be a most surprising villain. I wasn't getting an image of him as capable of being a criminal mastermind in this way," said Beav.

Serena thought about it. "Victor's profile would suggest that he is capable of doing anything, legal or illegal, if he believes it to be moral. When he killed those people, he did so accidentally. He was working on something that he believed would cure disease. Yes, he conducted experiments around the law, and those proved to be fatal. But you see what I'm saying?"

"We are looking for a cause," said Beav.

"Yes! Let's look into Victor's profile."

"Pulling it up now," said Lehman from his station a few feet away.

"What do you want me to do?" asked Nicholas.

"We need Victor's financial records, anything you can pull off his computers, anything you can find anywhere really," said Serena.

"You think that's what Erik was looking for?" asked Beav.

"I suspect Victor was hired by someone powerful, or someones powerful. If Erik could find out who that was, he wouldn't need Victor anymore," said Serena.

"Profile's up," called Lehman.

"I'm not seeing any— oh wait," said Beav. "He cited scientific misconduct as the reason why he worked outside of the system. He said that the system was corrupt, flawed, and too slow."

"OK then, so he doesn't trust the system. And he already knows that the vice president was in on the SM Channel security leak, spying, and whatever else they were doing with it. Isn't it possible that he assumed that President Kinji was also involved?" Serena stated this as a question but her voice indicated that she believed it as a fact.

Beav snapped his fingers. "So when he showed up in Kinji's office, he thought he was saving us all from... whatever it is that they are doing."

"Yes! I think so. I think he's actually trying to be heroic. Which means...he's on our side and if we can convince him of that, he'll help us," said Serena.

"Miss Serena? I found Victor's bank account. He has two of them," said Nicholas. "I'll put both up on the screen."

Serena clapped her hands together. "That was easy!"

Beav looked to see what she was so gleeful about and chuckled. There was only one form of income coming in, and the source was easy to identify: it was Uncle Sam.

"I think you're right about him. He's working for us, trying to seal that crack in the SM Channel, and he thinks we are the bad guys keeping it open," said Beav.

"I hate to burst your bubble, but why did Erik mention wanting to find who was paying him?" asked Lehman.

"Notice how Morgan got quiet and then uneasy. He wanted to get out at that point. He knew that Victor was on government payroll, and knew that Erik would eventually find out," said Serena.

"It's not quite adding up for me, but I think you are right: Victor will talk to us if he knows whose side we are on," said Beav.

"I think I know who can convince him," said Serena. "Nicholas, could you please send up another flare for Paul Tracy? I need his help again."

25

Paul Tracy knew that he'd hear from Serena Wilcox again, he was waiting for her call. He had been holding back on them – why shouldn't he? Nothing whatsoever had been offered to him, nothing at all, even though the crimes he was guilty of committing were acts that most Americans called him a hero for! Yet he had been thrown away to rot in prison with no concern for his welfare, and that was unacceptable. He stared at his digi watch, expecting that it would alert him of Serena's call any minute. When it finally did he took his sweet time in responding.

Nicholas warned Serena, "You better talk fast. When he answers I can only keep this line secure for five minutes, maybe ten."

Paul answered in a faux Southern drawl. "Hello? Is this by any chance my dear friend Serena Wilcox?"

"Paul, I need your help." Serena spoke quickly, in a vain attempt to minimize the effect that she knew the words 'I need your help' would have on Paul's ego.

"With?" If Serena could have seen him she would have seen that Paul wore a smile as wide as the Cheshire Cat's.

"I want to talk to Victor, but he doesn't trust us. If you talk to him, I think you can convince him to talk to me."

"Victor! Why Victor? It's me you want to talk to." Paul paced the cell, drawing attention from his fellow inmates on the block.

"Can you help us?" Serena dug deep within herself for patience.

"Yes and no."

"Yes and no?" She counted to ten.

"I can, but I won't until I get something in return."

"What do you want? You know we can't let you out of prison, that's not something I would even attempt to ask for." Serena glanced at Estep. If she was ready to snap, she knew he must be at his boiling point. She was surprised that he hadn't sparked off before now.

"I want privileges."

Estep interjected, "What kind of privileges?"

Here we go, thought Serena.

"I have certain requirements," he said.

"Dare I even ask what those are?" asked Serena.

"I want specific reading material."

"I don't want to hear more about his, will you help me or not?" Serena attempted to get the conversation back to a productive place.

"You don't even know what I want," said Paul.

"I don't want to hear about your tastes," said Serena.

"Why not? You probably like the same thing I do," said Paul.

"OK, that's enough!" snapped Estep.

"What did I say wrong? I want to read the

classics, like Watership Down and Les Miserable. All I get here is contemporary drivel, unless I read digital books on the SM Channel. I want a real book in my hands, one that smells like library dust and mildew. I would have thought you to be a bird of a feather, Ms. Wilcox."

"Ah, yes, sure." Serena breathed a sigh of relief. "I'll get your books. Now please help me, we are wasting time." That was twice now that she had assumed that a criminal was talking about something perverse when they weren't. Not that she wanted to let her guard down, but she was relieved that her investigation hadn't taken that kind of a turn.

"I need more than the books."

"Quick, tell me everything you want." Serena put her hands together and squeezed them as hard as she could. She had a sudden urge to punch something.

"I want visits from Vanessa," he said.

"Eew, there it is! I won't help with that." She released the grip she had on her hands and shook them wildly, like a little girl might do upon seeing a spider.

"I don't mean conjugal visits! I just enjoy

257

talking with her."

"We can do that," Lehman confirmed.

"And one more thing," Paul said mysteriously.

"What? Come on, Paul, we don't have much time!" Serena's voice took on a whiny quality that even her own ears didn't appreciate.

"Stay in touch. You need something, you call me. It's mind-blowing what I can find out from here," he said.

"We don't have time for this!" Estep bellowed.

"All right. I'll consider talking to Victor. But I'll do you one better. I'll tell you what I know. I was waiting until I could talk directly with you, Ms. Serena. Send everyone else out of there."

"This place, and actually yours as well I'm guessing, is wired. I can't give you privacy even if I wanted to," she said.

"OK then, at least I have your own ears listening to me directly."

Serena wasn't sure what he meant by this- her undivided attention maybe- but she didn't much care what he meant as long as he finally told her whatever it is he knew. "Yes, you do. Please, Paul, Nicholas is giving me the 2 minute warning."

"FYD is linked with big oil. They want Kinji

taken down – out – they want her dead." Now that he finally had something important to say Paul was speaking quickly, so fast that Serena had to strain to catch what he was saying.

"Who does? What else do you know? When? Where?" Serena threw all the questions out of her mouth as fast as she could.

"It's going down at the Global Oil Initiative."

"Anything you know – tell me, please!" As Serena ended her plea she heard Estep start to add something of his own. She spun around to face him and put a finger to her lips. The last thing they needed was for him to interrupt.

"Multiple nations are involved. Kinji won't cooperate with their agenda, but they know someone who will. They want her out, and the VP in."

"Paul, that can't be right. You must have seen President Kinji's announcement today, addressing the nation about Morgan's death." Serena's shoulders slumped in resignation, another dead end.

Paul spoke rapidly, as if not taking any time out to breathe. "Exactly. They took him out. His ex-wife was simply a ready volunteer to pull the trigger, don't waste your time on her. Lita knows insider information, but her interest was personal. Her sister's death, her love triangle-gone-wrong, yadda yadda yadda. Wrong tree. You want to look at who is replacing Morgan."

Serena asked, "They planned to take Morgan out all along?"

"No, not all along, only when he got cold feet and became a liability."

"And his replacement?" Estep jumped in, despite Serena's reproachful eyes.

Nicholas interrupted. "Thirty seconds, that's all I can do!"

"Quick—anything else?" Serena squealed.

"They already bought the person they want as VP, but I don't know who it is. That's all I know, for real this time," said Paul.

"20 seconds!" Nicholas yelled.

"You'll talk to Victor?" asked Serena, trying to use her remaining seconds to nail down what she wanted in the first place.

"My books, Vanessa, and you, my dear?"

"Yes, yes, and maybe."

"Maybe doesn't get you Victor." Paul adopted a British accent for no apparent reason.

"10 seconds!" Nicholas made a frantic wrap-it-up hand gesture.

"Yes," Serena blurted out.

"You'll call?" Paul verified in his natural voice.

"Yes, yes! Victor?" Serena was down to the wire now.

"Will do," said Paul at the last possible second.

Nicholas disconnected the signal. "Whew, that was close."

Serena exhaled with a prolonged sigh. "Talking to him stomped on my every last nerve, but wow, did he give us an earful!"

Lehman shook his head. "I'm not convinced that there is any validity to what Paul was saying. The office of vice-president won't be filled until President Kinji nominates a successor, and that person will only take office if approved by a majority vote in both houses of Congress."

"What if they already know who President Kinji would choose? Wouldn't that be something that insiders would know?" asked Serena.

"And they have paid off both the House and Senate? You're proposing a conspiracy that runs so deep and wide that it's taken over most of the United States government," said Beav. "Not that

I'm saying it couldn't happen, just saying it's quite a tale. I'm afraid Lehman could be right. Paul gave us bupkis."

They sat in collective silence, each of them letting their eyes wander about the room. The Superman lab was a beauty, to the extent that machines could be beautiful. While they admired the gleaming technology, Lehman jumped as if zapped by static electricity. He walked to the nearest station and brought up one of his favorite database sites. He pointed a finger at Serena and gestured for her to come closer.

Serena looked over his shoulder to see the screen. "What am I looking at?"

"I spoke too soon. I did a quick search of a media line archive feed. And look at what's popped up; fifteen results." Lehman turned around to face everyone.

"Results for what?" asked Beav.

Lehman summarized what he found. "President Kinji was quoted regarding the office of the vice presidency. She has been fairly open in the past about her displeasure that Morgan Canon was pushed on her as a vice presidential candidate. When pressed for who she preferred to have as a vice president she gave an honest answer-- Carson Landon-- and this was as recently as two weeks ago."

Beav wasn't convinced. "Even so, nothing will be resolved by the time of the GOB initiative that has been rescheduled to meet in about fourteen hours from now."

Nicholas suddenly appeared at Lehman's side. His eyes were wide open, which was the most expressive emotion any of them had seen the mild-mannered Nicholas display. "I don't know how this happened, but someone is asking for you from Paul's connection, and it isn't Paul."

"Asking for who? Me?" asked Serena.

"Yes, she wants to talk to you." Nicholas scurried back to his station with everyone close at his heels.

Serena bent over the desk and spoke directly into the microphone source, even though the sensitivity of the technology made such a move unnecessary. "Hello?"

"It's me, Lita." Her text message flitted across the screen. The text-to-audio function was locked.

"Lita! How did you get this connection?" Serena continued to use the microphone, on speaker mode so that the team could jump in at any time.

"Paul and I have a mutual acquaintance on his cell block who has been eavesdropping on Paul's conversations. He gave me Paul's security codes."

"How did he get those? He wouldn't have gotten them from eavesdropping," Lehman asked.

"He heard the audio tones, memorized the code. He passed a message along through my mother that Paul had you in his digi watch and that this line is secure."

"Vanessa has been to see Paul already?" Serena was amazed. They had reached that deal only seconds ago.

"No, she was there to see our mutual friend. I promised him I wouldn't tell you who he is. Let's get off of this. I am contacting you because I know some things. I hated Morgan, that's no secret, and I have no regrets – I'd do the same all over again."

"But?" Serena prompted. She had absolutely no idea where this was going. The surprise turn in the case had her adrenaline pumping – oh how she loved a mystery!

"But I do regret that I helped them."

"Them?" Serena could hardly wait for the answer, and she thought she knew what it was: Paul was right about all of it; everything he said was the truth.

"Morgan wasn't their choice to be president and I got rid of him for them. President Kinji isn't their choice either. You get what I'm saying."

"Yes, I follow you," said Serena.

"They talked to me through the SM Channel. They said no one could see what we were saying, but we could find each other if we knew our handles. And I want you to have them. I only have two of them, but that's all you need to find them."

"Why are you helping us, Lita?" asked Serena.

"Because they killed my sister, and they'll get me next."

Beav entered the conversation for the first time. "We'll get them before they get you, or the president. Give us the handles."

"I can trust all of the people in the room with you? Never mind, I have no choice. This is what you need. 45671 and 23987."

"She's disconnected the call." Nicholas immediately pulled up a chair alongside Lehman. "Let me help you find them."

Lehman and Nicholas spent the next half hour sifting through the dozens of secret conversations found in the hidden world inside the SM Channel. Beav and Serena followed along on the big monitor.

"Stop!" said Beav. "Right there! Look!"

And there it was, a conversation between the two handles 45671 and 23987, dialog that had been logged only twenty minutes before Paul Tracy spoke to them, a conversation he obviously saw with his own eyes because he quoted from it. These messages were in text form, audio files unavailable.

45671: "It's going down at the Global Oil Initiative."

23987: "I want assurances."

45671: "I can't do that. I've been told she'll name me as the VP selection at GOB. I can't verify it."

23987: "We need you in."

45671: "I know that."

23987: "We're down to a year. She won't be out of office before the agreement, she needs to be taken out."

45671: "I know, you've made yourself clear. I told you, I'm working on it."

23987: "The last guy we tapped got cold feet, and now his toes are tagged."

45671: "Don't threaten me."

23987: "I'm not. I'm telling you what will happen if you don't hold up your end of our arrangement."

45671: "I have no intention of backing out. I stand to benefit just as much as you do."

23987: "Good to know."

45671: "She contacted me right away. I don't think Morgan's body was even cold yet. No one will be surprised, she talked to the media about me a couple of weeks ago. All looks good."

23987: "Then what's the problem?"

45671: "I'm saying I can't guarantee it. She could change her mind last minute. I've done my part."

23987: "There's no one else she's even mentioned as a VP choice, no one but you."

45671: "Even so, I'm saying I can't guarantee it. I can only say that it looks like a done deal. She's announcing at the press conference at GOB."

23987: "That would be immediately following the initiative then."

45671: "I assume."

23987: "All interested parties will be at GOB."

45671: "I know that."

23987: "They expect to see you."

45671: "I'll be there."

23987: "In person meets are discouraged obviously, but they'll be watching you."

45671: "What are you telling me?"

23987: "Look sharp."

45671: "You contacted me. I told you all I know. What are you saying?"

23987: "Some don't trust you. Watch your back."

45671: "I told you that I'm on board. I've done all that you have asked. Are you telling me that they might kill me anyway?"

23987: "That's what I'm telling you."

45671: "I don't know what more I can do to gain their trust."

23987: "Turn up, be ready to give assurances."

45671: "I said I'd be there."

That was the last message transmitted. Serena said, "That leaves little doubt about what's going on."

"The good news is that it doesn't look like President Kinji is in immediate danger," said Lehman.

"The bad news is that multiple parties want her dead and we can't get to all of them. We're talking about entire nations declaring the assassination of our president," said Beav.

"We can start by making sure their guy doesn't make it to the office of the vice presidency," said Serena.

"We can flip him. He knows they might kill him, it would be easy." Estep's voice was difficult to hear because he was talking while moving around the room.

Lehman shot that idea down before it could take root. "Too risky, we can't trust him. He can't be allowed to work alongside President Kinji. We get him out, put someone we trust in. Keep President Kinji under heavy security at all times. That's the best we can do."

Serena nodded. "Agreed. After all, President Kinji lives with the threat of assassination every day. At least the GOB conspirators will suffer a setback when their puppet isn't selected."

"It will be satisfying to knock them off course for at least a little while." Estep wandered back to the station where the others were still gathered.

Serena raised her voice an octave and spoke in a teasing, sing-song rhythm that she used on her kids when she got them to do what she wanted. "If only we knew of someone to nominate for the office of the vice presidency, someone President Ann Kinji trusts with her most critical situations, trusts enough to pull out of retirement. Someone with a clean record free of scandal. Someone who is perhaps standing right in front of me."

Beav added, "Someone who is wearing a blue shirt."

"Oh no, no, no, no. Don't look at me," said Lehman. "She needs a governor or politician."

"That didn't work out so well, did it?" Serena reminded him. "She needs to look outside of the old boys' club."

"I'm going back to 'Bama." Lehman physically walked away, adding emphasis to his statement.

"Sure you are, to fetch your wife and pack your bags." Beav called out to Lehman's disappearing form, "Come on, you know you're going to do it!"

26

Lita was being held in a secured location near The Cube. Serena was thankful for the lapse in judgment that had allowed Lita to keep her digi pen. Thanks to this oversight, they now had the key information they needed. However, Serena knew that she would still benefit from talking to Victor, which is why she was headed for the prison for the criminally insane. Victor had already been returned there, deposited in his old cell.

There was no need for all of them to talk to

Victor; Lehman and Estep stayed behind in the Superman lab. Lehman continued slugging though the SM Channel logs with Nicholas while Estep kept an eye out for anything suspicious, when he wasn't going on food runs or nodding off in a chair. Time was also moving sluggishly for Beav and Serena who were on a short flight on a private plane – car travel was too much of a time-waster this close to the GOB initiative. Beav slept during their flight while Serena used the time to reflect on everything that had happened over the past few days.

How they had managed to keep everything quiet she didn't know, but the bomb scare in The Cube would, against all odds, remain a heavily guarded secret until after the GOB initiative. After that, every second of that harrowing ordeal would be analyzed. Serena could already think of something off the top of her head that would be a huge issue during the investigation: why hadn't they cleared the room before Beav diffused the bomb? At the very least, President Kinji should have been whisked away. Ah, a problem for a different day, she thought.

In Serena's mind Operation Covert Coffee was

wrapping up. Between whatever she would glean from Victor and whatever Lehman pulled off the computer (if anything), loose ends would be tied up within an hour or two. At that point, all that would remain would be the clean-up; explaining (some of, but never all of) what happened to the media and investigators, staying vigilant because the president's enemies were still too numerous to get rid of them all, keeping Carson Landon on their watch list and, while on the subject of vice presidential candidates, making sure that Lehman was the new VP.

Serena had helped find the biggest immediate threat to President Kinji, had flushed out several links in the conspiracy chain, and overall felt she had finished what she was hired, off record, to do. Soon all of the former agents and her own rouge self would be off payroll, and denied any further access to The Cube. Serena was more than ready! This was the longest she had ever been away from her kids. If she thought about that too long she knew that the tears would start flowing and she wouldn't be able to regain control of herself. Fortunately the plane touched down before her thoughts consumed her.

Serena learned that the FBI and Homeland Security had each had their go at Victor before their plane was even in the air, but Victor was talking to no one. She had a good feeling that she would be able to break his silence: Surely Paul had been effective in coaching Victor to trust her. She was banking on it.

Victor rose to greet Serena and Beav when they entered the room, causing three security guards to flinch. He sat back down. "We meet again," he said.

"Yes, under less stressful circumstances," said Serena. "I assume that Paul Tracy spoke to you on my behalf?"

"Yes he did."

"And you trust me?" asked Serena.

"I lack the ability to read social cues," he said.

Serena and Beav sat patiently, waiting for Victor to elaborate. Nearly sixty seconds dragged on before Serena gave up. "Are you willing to talk to me?"

"Yes, that's what I was implying. I failed to read social cues correctly and I erroneously aligned myself with the wrong side. My perception has 20/20 vision now due to the corrective lens gifted to me by Paul Tracy."

"You won't regret talking with me. I do have the best interests of this nation at heart," said Serena.

"I understand."

There was another awkward pause, in which Serena and Beav studied Victor. He was nothing like the garish portrayal that Erik's clown suit had given them, and yet, they could already understand why Erik was provoked to dish out such a mean-spirited parody. Anyone hoping to manipulate Victor into doing whatever they wanted would become frustrated. He had his own rigid set of rules that may or may not allow him to do whatever it was they wanted of him. Serena perceived that Erik had enjoyed the nasty impersonation of Victor because he had pushed his patience to the brink, and then over the edge. Talking with Paul Tracy was a delightful experience compared to the work required to get anything out of Victor. Serena was grateful that Agent Estep wasn't with them.

"What can you tell us about the work you were doing?" asked Serena.

"I can tell you everything." Victor sat across from them, arms hanging limply at his sides, his body slightly hunched over, his eyes cast downward. Eye contact was fleeting at best, at worst he studied the surface of the table in front of him as if he had forgotten that anyone else was in the room.

Serena and Beav waited. They looked at each other. Beav shrugged. They waited a few more seconds. Serena said, "Please tell us everything now."

"I agree to that. You will write everything down?" asked Victor.

"Everything you say is being recorded by the cameras in this room," said Beav.

"Technology can fail," said Victor simply.

"I will take notes," said Beav. He signaled to one of the guards who left the room briefly and returned with a notepad and a pencil that was as rounded as a preschooler's first writing instrument. No sharp instruments allowed, not even in the interrogation rooms.

"Shall we begin?" asked Serena.

"We shall," said Victor. "Do you want me to start at the beginning?"

"Yes, please do," said Serena. She willed herself to appear unhurried, completely patient,

Zen-like. She hoped they got everything they could out of Victor before she lost it.

"We teamed up over mutual hatred, Lita and me, but that's not the beginning, that's the ending. The beginning is what you want."

"Yes, please continue." Serena smiled sweetly.

"In the beginning I was a scientist. I was doing a good job, and one day there was a problem. I knew that there was fraud. They were taking my findings and recording the data differently from the truth. I knew I had to stop them, and I did. Then I had to face trial for what I had done and I went here. I met Paul Tracy and Vanessa. They were my friends. Vanessa told the FYD that I would do what they wanted. She was helping me get out of here."

"That's when Morgan Canon and Erik Chapman were visiting her?" Serena wanted to clarify every point that cross-referenced testimony they already had.

"Yes. Morgan is dead."

"That's right. He was killed by Lita."

"That's what Lita wanted. I wanted it too."

"Why did you want Morgan dead?" Serena opened a door that she hoped would lead them toward something useful, but she risked falling down a rabbit hole. Fortunately Victor wasn't one to grandstand pointlessly as Paul was so fond of doing, so wherever he was taking them, he would get them there fast.

"I hated him because he lied to me. I created the crack in the SM Channel as he requested. He told me that the hidden room in the Channel was for the purpose of discussing top secret research in the area of mind control, the very area he knew I had been assigned to before I was arrested and put on trial. He deceived me."

"What was the crack really used for?" asked Beav.

"It was a water cooler for liars and cheats. They spun their webs of deceit in the safe place I myself created for them, to make a mockery of science for their own gain. They were gathering data to manipulate it. What they couldn't alter they buried. Who they couldn't bribe, they threatened. They bought and bullied their way to the very top. They told me that they had President Ann Kinji on their side, but I understand now that they lied to me about that. President Kinji was never involved, and I see that now. Paul Tracy showed me how they are plotting against her. It went as high up as Morgan

Canon, and now they want to replace him with another they can control."

"I think we can head that off, but we need as much information from you as possible. What can you tell me about who they are? What kind of research are they most interested in?" asked Serena.

"They have an interest in genetically engineered foods. The interest is of course financial, with a complete and utter disregard for science or ethics. I suppose you have an opinion about genetically engineered foods?"

Serena was caught off guard. She studied Victor's expression, which was difficult because his face was unnaturally blank. She tried to guess what a mind like his would want to hear. "I don't know what opinion I should have. I don't have the research to look at."

Victor appeared quite satisfied by her answer. He launched into a quote: " 'Science is built up of facts, as a house is built of stones; but an accumulation of facts is no more science than a heap of stones a house.' Jules-Henri Poincare, who died in 1912, before you were born."

"Yes, before I was born. And you as well." Serena felt like she had fallen down a rabbit hole that had many more holes left inside it to fall through.

"The ingestion of genetically engineered food is not harmless, the genetically engineered materials are neither completely destroyed by stomach acids nor is this material prevented from reaching the bloodstream. Blood cells are also affected, as the body is incapable of preventing access. Toxins are in the food, toxins are then in the human body, including carcinogens. We cannot alter the foods without altering the human body. New proteins produced in genetically engineered foods are capable of acting as toxins or allergens in and of themselves, not to mention altering the nutritional value of the food through mutations. You mentioned research. Of course we don't have research, not of the long-term sort. Genetically engineered foods have flooded the market and continue to do so in great numbers, all without any hard data on its effect on humans. I am dumbing this down for you the best that I can."

"I appreciate that," said Serena.

"The GE projects dovetail the mind control projects. You see, when food is genetically altered and allowed to cause mutation in the human body, the concept of human DNA is now open to manipulation, interpretation, redefinition, recreation. Ethically, there are concerns, quite naturally, if one were to follow through with that line of thinking. 'Science without religion is lame, religion without science is blind.' Albert Einstein."

"You believe that genetically engineered foods are unethical and you voiced objection?" Serena ventured to guess. Usually she was quick to get into someone's head but Victor's mind was slippery.

"No, not at all. I haven't reached a conclusion yet. However, I object to motivation for advancement in research being greed. Large corporations stand to gain significantly, as do governments, both foreign and domestic. Gone is the scientist. Gone is the truth. Here is the false data. Here is the lottery ticket."

"I understand what you are saying. And at this point you said you wanted to stop helping them?" Serena tried to steer the conversation toward a resolution, if there was one.

"No. I was promised I would have access to my old research and I would even be given research privileges to continue with my work."

"Your work with the mind control project?"

"Yes. The two areas had become connected, and there were hungry parties bearing down on me to have my data. I knew this, and yet I believed that the end justified the means. My work in mind control was to be a contribution to science like no other. I was of the delusion that I could prevent nations, corporations and individuals from altering human DNA against one's will by getting my hands on the science first. One step ahead of evil, one step ahead of corruption. I am a protector of science and a preserver of that which is human. I have sworn an oath."

"An oath? Are you a part of an organization?" Beav asked.

Victor looked at him uncomprehendingly.

"Did you swear an oath literally?" Beav tried again.

"I swore an oath of my own."

"Like a superhero might do?" Serena was pleased with herself for intuiting at least a little bit about what made Victor tick.

"Yes! A person of science is held to a self-standard. 'You cannot hope to build a better world without improving the individuals. To that end each of us must work for his own improvement, and at the same time share a general responsibility for all humanity, our particular duty being to aid those to whom we think we can be most useful.'"

"Marie Curie!" Serena had a Marie Curie T-shirt, a side note she doubted would impress Victor.

"Well done. I hold myself accountable, being tasked with a mind that can delve into the mysterious unknown quicker and with greater grasp than this present generation. I am charged with a responsibility, a heavy weight, to protect and serve mankind." Victor's hair fell loosely about his forehead and was now dangling over his left eye. He didn't seem to notice.

"And you believe that by discovering the secrets you can then find a way to protect mankind from harm?" Serena was distracted by the hair over Victor's eye. Didn't that bother him? She resisted the temptation to reach over and push the hair away from his face, knowing that touching him would be a very bad idea.

"Yes, you understand me exactly."

"Please explain how your research led to the situation you find yourself in now," said Beav. He intended to let Serena lead, but this question was too pressing to keep to himself.

"Are you familiar with Synthia, the first so-called artificial life form created by Craig Venter, a billionaire entrepreneur? That was back when the field of 'synthetic biology' was in its infancy. NASA's researchers warned of hackers with the ability to engineer viruses or bacteria to control human minds, with genetic engineering the next frontier of computing. And indeed we are seeing the beginnings of such mayhem. To quote Hessel, 'I advocate that cells are living computers and DNA is a programming language.' He went so far as to say 'I want to see life programmed and used to solve global challenges so that humanity can achieve a sustainable relationship within the biosphere.' The danger of course is that 'viruses and bacteria send chemicals into human brains and could be used to influence, or even 'control' their host.' Fast forward a few short years, and we've arrived. We are already doing this, doing it as we speak."

Victor paused to take a sip of water which had been recently set before him via a plastic cup. Then he resumed, his pitch reflecting no emotion, but his eyes finally showing signs of life.

"Synthetic biology led to new forms of bioterrorism, already in the works as you probably heard about. A simple vaccine could do the trick, and there's our mind control, all ripe for bio-terrorism, a plot discovered only a week or so ago in fact—effectively prevented, but you see how narrow the escape was. As the technology advances, one day the hackers-of-the-mind will succeed. The body itself, our very own DNA, is not the next generation computer, but the computer of today, right now. Trust me, we are already there, and have been close for the past decade. Forget drones and global listening devices, we are getting literally inside people's heads. Let me make myself clear: we are already doing this."

"It's a lot to take in. And honestly, you're scaring me. I don't think I'll sleep for a week." Serena meant it. She wished she could take back the past few minutes of her life and not hear any of what he just said.

"Awareness is key."

"I'm not sure we need to know any more details about your research, only how it relates to the multiple conspiracies we are dealing with, and any information you can give us that can protect the president," said Beav, again attempting to zero in on what they needed to know.

"I laid down the foundation for that. You see, the mind control project is funded by the genetic engineering project and vice versa. The two are entwined and benefit much of the same people. The deal on the table with GOB is what they are protecting. Global Oil Bank has packaged a world-wide initiative to aid developing nations in the technologies to end world hunger and the conservation of resources. Naturally we look to big oil with this situation, as well as the nations who export the most oil. All fingers are in the pie. If you look to the lobbyists who have the most influence, you'll see that all of them have a stake in what's happening with GOB. Corn, food of any kind, it's all in line to profit. Food industry and oil industry have combined forces and are unbeatable. They have become so power hungry that they will take down the presidency to guarantee that they will get their initiative. And no one cares that their dabbling with genetics indirectly via our food supply will eventually render us into something not quite human, at least not composed of the human DNA we know today. Not to mention the ramifications of deliberately and directly altered DNA via vaccines or other vessels for the purpose of mind control or information retrieval."

"This sounds horrific and hopeless!" Serena wailed.

"No, not hopeless. Without much hope is more accurate. My appearance in President Kinji's office with a threat to detonate a bomb was my attempt to pre-empt the situation. I thought Kinji herself had been bought. I planned to disrupt the GOB and send the nation into chaos. I understand now that I was wrong about Kinji, and that my plan had no guarantee of serving as a large enough disruption to throw the GOB off track. However, I do have a better plan now that I know the truth."

"What plan is this?" asked Beav.

"Spy on the crack in the SM Channel. They don't know you can see in," said Victor. "With me out of the way, they will assume that they have use of it indefinitely."

"Already doing that, yes," said Serena.

"Good. Here is the heart of my plan. Promise me you will carry it through, deliver it to President Kinji."

"I can try." Serena nodded.

"It's critical for the future of mankind. Surely you can do better. While I was prepared to die for this cause, you can't be troubled to pass along a message?"

"I'll pass along your message. Please go on," said Serena.

"I have your word?"

"You have my word." Serena extended her hand for Victor to shake it, but he only looked at the hand. She let her arm drop.

"Listen carefully. Set up a body of ethical scientists as a watchdog over GOB. I know that there are pre-existing task forces and ethics-in-science organizations, but we need something new, something powerful, something now! Put the spotlight on GOB, expose them to the light! Get the media on it! Get everyone on it! Expose the crack in the SM Channel and let the entire world see their lie!" Victor suddenly showed emotion, and he almost moved his body. But this spark, this rare connection, was to be short lived.

"Excellent! I definitely agree. Do you have any names you can suggest? Any colleagues?" Serena asked.

"Why Albert of course, and Marie Curie. Females have brought a new voice to the field..."

"You do know that Albert Einstein and Marie

Curie are long dead, right?" asked Serena, not sure she wanted to know the answer.

"Of course, of course," Victor muttered. He looked dazed for a few seconds and then he started writing numbers in the air with his index finger. He got up and shuffled about the room, mumbling to himself and writing in the air. The guards watched him closely but didn't interfere.

"We'll let ourselves out," said Serena.

Victor didn't acknowledge that she said anything.

"Wait, wait!" Serena doubled back to the table. "Victor, please focus! Do you hear me? Victor? Victor?"

Victor halted his steps but continued to mumble and draw numbers.

"Please, Victor. I thought of something. What do you know about The Supporters? They are a group of mathematicians. They seem to be on our side. What do you think of them? Victor?"

Victor seemed to snap back to reality as if he had never left it. He waltzed back to his chair, sat down and said, "Oh yes, I know them. The Supporters would make a fine watchdog group. They have been doing so on a volunteer basis without any real resources. They would appreciate a call, yes."

"Do you know how I can get in touch with them?" asked Serena.

"Use the word Supporters in any conversation in the crack in the SM Channel. Best to drop the name twice so they know you didn't mention them inadvertently."

"Then they'll tell us where to find them?"

"No. They'll find you."

27

"It's time to face the nation," said President Ann Kinji. "I have a lot of explaining to do, but I'll let my gifted people do all of that background. What I need to do is reassure America that I'm still effectively leading this country, all while also telling them that I've lost control of the presidency."

"Were you ever really in control of the presidency? Has anyone been?" asked Serena. "I'm not being facetious. You aren't Queen Kinji or

Madam Dictator Kinji. Last I knew, this was still America and you are but one person in a body of government. Throughout history American presidents have had strained relationships with their government family. This is nothing new, and that's what you need to tell yourself."

"No American president has ever had this situation."

"I imagine the Civil War days were dicey. President Ann, I know it feels unprecedented, but is anything on this Earth ever really 'new'?"

"I hear what you are saying. So what did past presidents do?"

Serena strode swiftly across the room to her dear friend and President of the United States and gave her a strong bear hug; one squeeze and a quick release. "They gave American people hope for the future." Serena dug her digi pen out of her purse and began scribbling away.

"What are you doing?"

"I'm looking up a quote. And I found it already!" She selected speaker mode on the digi and a female voice said, "President Abraham Lincoln, July 28, 1862, 'I shall not do more than I can, and I shall do all I can to save the government, which is my sworn duty as well as my personal inclination. I shall do nothing in malice.' See? You aren't the only president to feel that government needed saving. And yet here we are, you and me, standing on top of the presidential seal."

"I don't suppose I can plagiarize what the American greats have said?"

"You'll figure it out. It wouldn't hurt to mention the name of God."

"Religion and politics don't mix."

"Religion and politics are always conjoined. Trying to separate the two gives us a fractured nation; one half without a heart and the other without a brain."

Ann laughed. "Well I certainly can't say that!"

"I look forward to hearing your speech. I'm so honored when you bounce things off of me, but you never need anyone's help as far as I can see."

"You don't follow politics and you haven't stayed current with government issues."

"Ouch."

"I like the fresh perspective. If I were to strip away the insular world of The Cube, what would the United States look like?" Ann opened her arms in sweeping gesture.

"I'm an independent and an idealist. Everyone has their bias."

"Independent thinking and idealism – we need more of that. You help me a great deal." President Kinji held the door open for Serena, the only cue that their conversation was over.

Serena squeezed her arm as she walked past the door. "God bless you."

Ann's expression softened and, to her own surprise, her eyes misted.

As Serena was escorted down the long corridor by two agents she called over her shoulder, "His name means something, doesn't it?"

Ann waved and closed her door. In two hours she would be addressing the nation. Her speech would make history books, one way or another. This was one of those rare open windows in time, in which one person's voice held the attention of the entire world. What would she do with that power, that awesome responsibility? Thoughts tumbled inside her mind, none of them productive or fruitful. She couldn't grasp hold of anything that felt right. She bit the tops off of three erasers before she was aware of what she was doing. Not knowing what to do, she found herself praying.

It wasn't a complicated prayer, just a general shout-out thought: "Please God, show me what to do." Then she immediately felt so sleepy that she could barely keep her eyes open. She lie down on the lounger near the mammoth SM Channel screen and instantly fell asleep. She woke only ten minutes later feeling refreshed and inspired. She spent the next fifteen minutes writing the speech of a lifetime. Ahead of schedule, she even had time to peel and eat an orange before her staff notified her that it was time to go.

At the podium, President Kinji commanded respect. Her eyes reflected unmistakable intelligence, her stance projected confidence. Her natural beauty and humor were the scale-tipping ingredients that won America's hearts. They hung on every word she said because she was a celebrity, but today they listened to her for reasons beyond her charisma and popular appeal; today they needed her to be their president.

"Dear Americans, what an earful you have had! I'm so sorry for the hand we've been dealt. The loss of a vice president is bad enough, but the conspiracy surrounding his death is a terrible blow. I'm pleased that my appointee has been warmly accepted, and I'd love to discuss him further, but today I have other things to talk about.

I need to talk to you about ideas that go beyond policy and governing. Before I get into that, let me bring you back to a time when policy and governing was the gut reaction to a dark time in not-so-distant American history when there was a spree of massacres. The horror of such events led lawmakers to create new legislation that would arm all active duty military personnel while off duty; they were, in fact required to take an oath similar to that of a medical doctor. If the public was threatened by violence, they must act.

The logic was that our military had the training to respond quickly to violent situations in public places, much like the role of an air marshal on an airplane. It was also said that our military is to protect not only our interests abroad, but must protect us here at home as well. And this logic did indeed hold up. The incidence of massacre when down to, well, near zero. Even plans to commit such a horrific act of violence seemed to be statistically low. So the reaction was a success, no?

No. Unfortunately, you may recall that following the lull in violent acts there was an extreme uptick in murder-suicides in private homes, where of course no armed member of the armed forces was protecting citizens. The hatred, madness and despair simply diverted itself to places where no one could stop them. There was even a coordinated effort for multiple murder-suicides to transpire on the same date, effectively creating private mass murder events that rivaled the numbers of victims from all the previous public massacres combined!

It was only when churches stepped forward and offered free counseling, when schools addressed bullying and other related issues, and when American citizens banded together that the violence began to subside. I don't know how much credit to give the publishing and entertainment industry for policing themselves, and the American public for the reversal of the popularity of violent media, as well as other hard-to-quantify social factors. I know that the picture is complex, and that I would be naïve if I thought I could summarize this in a few moments of musing.

But my point is that policy didn't improve the bleak situation. Policy didn't prevent murderous hearts from festering, sated only after spilling the blood of their fellow citizens. While it's difficult to understand all the pieces of the puzzle, what we can clearly see is that it was the American people themselves who turned things around. Think of the many stories of heroism following the tragedies, think of the stories of strangers helping strangers for months – even years—after the tragedies, think of the kindness of ordinary citizens as they found one simple way they could make a difference.

We have a very recent example of American ingenuity and kindness coming together to make a difference. I was overwhelmed when you dedicated my beautiful garden sanctuary to me, the ribbon cutting ceremony will remain one of my most cherished memories. And best of all, when I challenged you to ride that momentum of generosity and apply it to Americans who need it, The New America Foundation was created. In addition, citizens acted independently to help and serve America's neediest towns and cities.

During those wonderful occasions our differences were set aside and we were truly as one nation, although simmering underneath we were still a polarized country. Never fully leaving our awareness was the unfortunate truth that we remain a divided nation. And yet, this is nothing new. A friend of mine reminded me of an American president who governed our nation way before my time. What nation could be more divided than a country actively engaged in Civil War?

Yes, I'm talking about Abraham Lincoln, a president quoted so often that it's become cliché. And yet, I feel a kinship with this icon, this man we know only through history books. Lincoln said something that I really took to heart. What I just mentioned earlier, about how the American people turned things around by their own initiative, was also a hint at something else the American people tapped into: Goodness. And that's where my Lincoln quotes come in.

Now keep in mind that I am using these quotes out of context to make my own point. I encourage you to do your own study of Lincoln if you wish for these quotations to remain in their original intent and context. However, having said that, I hope that I am correct in believing that Lincoln would give me his blessing to use his words today.

July 31, 1846: 'That I am not a member of any Christian Church, is true; but I have never denied the truth of the Scriptures; and I have never spoken with intentional disrespect of religion in general, or of any denomination of Christians in particular.'

January 2, 1863: 'But I must add that the U.S. government must not, as by this order, undertake to run the churches. When an individual, in a church or out of it, becomes dangerous to the public interest, he must be checked; but let the churches, as such take care of themselves.'

August 26, 1863: 'Let us diligently apply the means, never doubting that a just God, in his own good time, will give us the rightful result.'

And finally, on October 24, 1863: 'Nevertheless, amid the greatest difficulties of my Administration, when I could not see any other resort, I would place my whole reliance on God, knowing that all would go well, and that He would decide for the right.'

Abraham Lincoln's words give me assurance that my response to our current state of confusion and mistrust is on the right path. It is not my intention to disrespect any religion, belief, or freedom to reject religion. It is also not my intention to lead churches. However, like Lincoln, I too wish to defer to a Higher Power.

There are times of darkness that logic alone

cannot address, when policy and governing have limitations. While I am at risk of offending you, may I suggest that you equate God with Love? What a beautiful world it would be if we were all in agreement that kindness makes a difference; that government can't fix all the things that are broken, things like the human heart. But you, my dear Americans, you have this power within you. If you are a praying person, please pray for our nation.

If you are offended by the very notion of prayer, please respect the freedom of others to pray, for prayer is a petition for help. Do not mix religion and politics. If I will agree to be a leader who stays out of church affairs, may I ask that you agree to stay out of the rights and freedoms of others to worship as they choose?

Stop fighting each other. Let statues stand, let people pray, let flags fly. Agree that Love is more important than settling who is right. When I close with my final words, may you hear them not with contempt or division in your heart, but with the goodness I wish for you; to be well, stay safe, fill your heart with hope, and love one another.

And these, my final words: God Bless America."

28

"Lehman, predictably, accepted President Kinji's Vice Presidential appointment, so we are on our own," said Beav.

"They'll never vote him in," said Estep.

Serena smirked. "Au Contraire! They've already agreed. Kinji mentioned that if anyone refused to sign off on the appointment, he or she would have to give her a plausible reason for why Lehman is not suited for the office-- or else she would explore their reason for bias; dig into their affiliations with lobbyists for example."

"Which means, like I said, we are on our own," said Beav.

Estep said, "I'm not in the loop. Isn't Operation Covert Coffee a completed mission? I've been reassigned to something else."

Serena filled him in. "We are wrapping things up, yes, but we need to get a few loose ends tied up. Obviously we can't hunt down every person who wants Kinji out of office, that would be a long list. Nor should we seal the crack. As you know, Operation Dumbo has begun." She noticed Estep's bewildered look. "Dumbo was the flying elephant with the big ears in the classic Disney film. Don't look at me, I didn't name it. Anyway, they have a team who is listening in on the crack in the SM Channel."

"Yes, I know. I wasn't assigned to the team because I was told I was still needed by you," said Estep, not without a dramatically resentful tone in his voice.

Serena ignored his theatrics. "We need to find the Supporters."

"Rather, we need to meet them. It seems they've seen our flare," said Beav. He pulled up the message for the three of them to examine together.

"It says for Serena to come alone, with no ears, not even a digi pen. I don't like it," said Estep.

"I have an idea," said Serena. "What if I wore a digi watch like Paul has? It's not common knowledge that prisoners have these, and they aren't available outside the prison population."

"That could work," said Beav.

"Unless they know someone in prison," said Estep.

"They'll scan me for bugs. The watch won't set anything off. If they don't know it's a digi I will pass their screen. You really think the odds are high that they know about the watch?" said Serena.

"No, I think it's a good risk. We can't send you in there with nothing," said Estep.

"Why won't they approve of me going with you? I already met with one of them once in Germany," said Beav.

"I don't know, but they said no and I think we should do what they want," said Serena. "They are on our side, remember? Beav said they are an organization of MENSA people, mathematicians mainly."

"Smart genius types have never been deranged

and violent?" said Estep

"I don't think this group is something to fear," said Beav.

"Agreed, I have a good feeling about this," said Serena.

"We better get moving," said Estep. He signaled to his team via an old school radio cuff. "Bluebird is on the move."

"Bluebird?" asked Serena.

"You," said Estep. "You're my new assignment. Operation Bluebird."

Beav's laugh began as a snorting sound and developed into an all-out guffaw.

"Laugh it up. My bonus for protecting Ms. Bluebird is paying for new tires for my car," said Estep.

The three of them set out together, joined by Agent Bonifield and Agent Champlin. They drove in two separate sedans and maintained a mostly silent journey for the entire two hour trip from Chicago to a rural stretch of road in Indiana. Upon arrival they all got out to stretch their legs and breathe the Hoosier air. Row after row of corn went on as far as the eye could see, and since the farmland was entirely flat, with barely any discernible slope, the Supporters could easily be anywhere. They could be watching them right now from only a few feet away, completely camouflaged. The three agents, and one former agent, were well aware of this possibility. While each of them had served in war zones, and all had been in situations of high pressure, it was the corn that struck their hearts with terror.

Serena's digi watch lit up. "Estep, who knows this number?"

"No one." He grabbed her arm. The watch, too big for her wrist, slid down her hand and fell onto the ground. "Don't pick it up!"

"Shouldn't I answer it? What if it's them?"

Serena didn't know how to answer the call on the digi watch so after a few seconds of fumbling with it Beav grabbed the watch. He knew exactly what to do because, like most contemporary government projects, he had been involved in the design of it.

"Hello?" she said.

"We wanted you to come alone, and without communication."

"Sorry, I couldn't do that."

"We expected as much."

"Then why did you even ask it of me?"

"It cut back on how much we have to deal with. All you have is the watch, correct?"

"Yes. How did you know about it?"

"One of us was in prison. But don't worry, we aren't violent."

"How did you get the number?"

"They are all coded in a series. We tried several until one went through."

Serena racked her brain to think of more ways to stall, more hints about who they were, anything! "Where are you?" She looked around her, as if expecting them to pop out in front of her from behind the corn stalks.

"Leave the watch behind, no tracking devices. Enter the corn row immediately in front of you. Keep moving down the row until you see an arrow on the ground. Follow the arrow. No agents. If anyone is with you, we will leave without meeting with you."

"Maybe we should call off the meeting. If you were honestly trying to help you would have no issue with federal agents I can personally vouch for."

"No agents – those are our terms."

"I can't agree to that."

The line was disconnected.

At that moment they heard the sound of tires crunching over gravel. Everyone watched as a government issue sedan slowed and then stopped a few yards from where they were gathered. The back door opened and a man exited the vehicle, a man they all recognized instantly as Carson Landon. They all stood stock still with their jaws dropping as they watched him walk toward them. He was unhurried, taking care to protect his $700 loafers.

"Is that who I think it is?" Serena asked rhetorically.

Carson held his hand out to her. "Carson Landon."

Serena stumbled over what to say. "How? How did you find us and what are you doing here?" She looked around her at the faces of everyone on the team—all looked completely baffled by Governor Landon's sudden appearance. She reached out to accept his handshake, but found something already in his hand.

"That should explain what I'm doing here. The 'how I found you' part is easy: we've had a tracer on your car." Carson pointed to the car that had been assigned to Agent Estep. "I have to say, you ruined my undercover work. The agents who recruited me are not happy. If one government hand would talk to the other every now and then we'd avoid these things."

Serena examined the object in her hand: a single sheet of paper folded several times over. She unfolded it and saw Paul's familiar handwriting. "One of the missing pages from Paul's journal!"

"Yes, this is the page that they didn't want you to see. Paul sent me a message telling me where to find his journal. He suggested that I keep this page in case I needed it." Carson folded his arms across his chest and waited for Serena to read the journal entry.

She addressed the entire team. "You'll need to verify this of course, but I can tell that the page I'm holding is from Paul's journal. He writes, 'The governor is working undercover. This will probably cost him politically. I wouldn't be surprised if I have him as a cellmate one day, but he's the only one that could pull this off I suspect. Nice to know there are good guys left in politics after all, although Carson Landon should have been VP. They'll find out that Morgan Canon was a big mistake. By then, it could be too late. I'm doing my part to write everything down. I will ask to speak with Serena Wilcox when the time is right. Until then, I'll continue reporting what I see, and I'll let the Supporters know about the governor's involvement.' He signed it and dated it. This was from over a month ago."

Carson cut an attractive figure against the backdrop of the orange sunset sitting on the rural horizon, a view completely unobscured by buildings or even trees. As far as the eye could see there was nothing but farmland, corn, and blue sky that was beginning to darken. Carson stood tall in his crisp navy suit and slim coordinating silk tie. His hair blew in the gusts of wind that sporadically came and went, looking like a male model posing for a calendar cover. Carson, the assembled team, and the government sedans were all in disharmony with the farm scene.

Beav, never intimidated by powerful people, asserted himself. "What is your connection to the Supporters?"

Carson frowned. "I'm not affiliated with the Supporters, but I know who they are, and that's why I'm here. You need to stay away from them."

"Tell us about them," said Serena.

"They are vigilantes who don't believe that government can police itself. While we want the same things, we disagree about how to make those things happen. I work within the system..." Carson let his sentence dangle while he shrugged.

"And they don't. I see. You came all this way to warn us about them?" Serena fixated on the sinking sun behind him. Soon they would be standing amongst the corn in complete darkness, not a house around for miles.

Carson launched into a speech. "Morgan Canon is obviously out of the picture—I do know what happened, by the way, and I even know what almost happened. Beav, I know who you are, and what you did. Thank you for your service. I know you can't be reinstated, but I'd like to thank you on behalf of all Americans, and if there's anything I can do for you, let me know. As far as I'm concerned my role is done, and so is yours. President Kinji is well satisfied with what you did, and she specifically requested that none of you run this thing so far into the ground that you dig up new problems. You got lucky. None of you were hurt. But it could have gone either way."

Estep didn't know if he should refute the claim or let it slip away unchallenged. He settled for a response that was somewhere in the middle. "Are you saying that you were working for President Kinji all along?"

Carson nodded slowly, a gesture that irked Estep. Carson did his best to smooth the team's ruffled feathers. "Don't take it personally guys. President Kinji needed you and you were there for her. I was on a parallel team, the official one. You see, there needs to be some, shall we say 'discretion', in how details are recorded, reported and investigated. For example, as you probably already guessed, it is better for the president that former agents are ghosts. That was, after all, what you signed up for. Covert Coffee needs to go dark. And, actually, it's time for Covert Coffee to end--- when the Supporters came up on my radar I came here to close the operation in person, before you peel a new layer of the onion."

Serena extended her hand to Carson; this time his hand was free of paper and he shook it. "Thank you for telling us this in person."

"Of course. Again, thank you on behalf of all Americans. While they may never learn what it is that you did to protect President Kinji and our nation, those of us who know what you did will certainly forever appreciate your service." Carson flashed them the smile of a man who might one day run for president and spun on heels the best he could on dry husks of corn. He strode to where his driver had been waiting, his shoes somehow managing to make a clicking sound, unless Serena imagined that sound.

As soon as the governor's car was out of sight and the team was preparing to head out themselves, the Supporters called. The voice on the line said, "Serena, take me off speaker. And hold the watch to your ear."

Serena looked at Estep and Beav. Neither objected. At this point, what would it hurt to hear him out the rest of the way? Besides, the longer they kept the line open the easier it would be for agents, the officially active ones, to catch them. Agent Bonifield and Agent Champlin indicated that they were paying attention.

Serena pressed the watch to her ear. "You're off speaker."

"Mommy!" An unmistakably familiar voice rang out, there were a few seconds of dead air, and then the call was disconnected.

A chill went through Serena's body and her fingers struggled to hold the watch. Her face froze. Her mind was a carnival of lights and sounds, but she willed herself into control. First, steady yourself. You can't let the team know that you heard the voice of your baby girl.

Serena gave the watch to Beav. Estep noted her expression and said, "What did he say to you?"

"I'm supposed to go in there, in the corn, to meet with them. I need to go alone."

Estep shook his head. "They said more than that to shake you up this much."

"The digi watch gave me a jolt when I had it next to my ear. Static electricity or something, still feeling it," said Serena.

Beav's eyebrows shot up in an unspoken question. Serena answered with a scowl. This exchange went unnoticed by the others who were already peering through the corn for any sign of the Supporters, but Beav understood her perfectly: don't say anything.

"I'm going in there now. Don't follow me; they won't talk to me if you do."

"I don't feel good about this," said Estep. "The

governor made it clear that Covert Coffee is over, and the order to desist came down from President Kinji."

Beav jumped in, "The official team, as the governor called it, still wants the Supporters. She can at least get the ball rolling for them while we're here. If she doesn't come out in fifteen minutes we'll go after her."

"Five. Daylight's all but gone," said Estep.

"Split the difference—ten. Give me ten minutes before you go in." Serena didn't wait for an answer but disappeared into the corn.

Estep timed Serena's absence to precisely five minutes. "That's it, we're going in."

Beav grasped Estep by the arm and pulled him away from the team. "Unless you have any objections I'd like to lead."

"Beav, what's going on? Covert Coffee is over, you know that. You can't be reinstated. Let's get Serena and move on." Estep shined a light into the blackness of the corn, illuminating nothing but corn and mud.

"Covert Coffee has become Operation Bluebird Flown." Beav added his light to Estep's, doubling the glare on the cornfield.

"No need for a mission. I'll get her home in time to watch the late show if you stop holding me back."

"No, she's long gone," said Beav.

"What are you talking about?" Estep stopped dead in his tracks.

"He was lying. Check with President Ann. Carson Landon was in the crack in the SM Channel, I don't have to tell you that." Beav looked back at the row of government vehicles; all was quiet.

"He said he was working undercover." Estep said slowly, the words forming in his mouth as his brain ferreted out the truth. "But no one checked his story." Estep bolted into the corn.

Beav, a runner, was smaller and lighter than Estep. He navigated the corn rows easily. He snagged the back of Estep's shirt and yanked him to a stop. "Wait! Let me lead this. I can't be reinstated, my career is over anyway. You can walk away from this right now."

Estep turned to face Beav. "Why did you let her go in there? What else aren't you saying?"

"They have her family."

COVERT COFFEE

EPILOGUE

As Serena Wilcox travels through the cornfield into the hands of the Supporters, Operation Covert Coffee has ended, and Operation Bluebird Flown has begun. The Covert Coffee team has not yet been named in a debriefing or in the media. Therefore President Ann Kinji extends the team's off-the-books contracts. All but Lehman, who has agreed to step in as Kinji's new vice president, are available to take on Bluebird Flown, the mission to find Serena Wilcox (again).

Agent Estep has taken to referring to Serena by the name "Serena Waldo" due to how often he is charged with finding her. Beav, now in his second back-to-back mission with Estep, has settled into the role of being Estep's partner, even though he can't be officially reinstated. Estep meanwhile is distracted by his girlfriend's ultimatum: the job or her. As if Estep wasn't short-fused enough, he is pushed to the limit when he must reconnect with the criminally insane club: Paul, Victor, and the mother-daughter duo Vanessa and Lita.

The layers of conspiracy that were peeled back in COVERT COFFEE expose the evil beneath in BLUEBIRD FLOWN, coming to you in fall 2013.

Look for Serena Wilcox Mystery #6

Bluebird Flown

Fall of 2013

The Serena Wilcox Mysteries
By Natalie Buske Thomas

Gene Play
Virtual Memories
Camp Conviction
Angels Mark
Covert Coffee
Bluebird Flown

Stay in the loop!

Twitter: @writernbt
Pinterest: writernbt
Facebook: Natalie Buske Thomas
www.nataliebuskethomas.com

ABOUT THE AUTHOR

Natalie Buske Thomas has authored six books and is a contributing author for four books. Natalie is also an artist and entertainer. Her oil paintings *Savannah Reading in the Butterfly Garden, Life Sustaining* and *Ron and Joy Before the War* have been on public exhibit.
Natalie sings, plays the drums and is a dancer. She performs on occasion with her family at nursing homes and community events.

Natalie is on Facebook, Twitter, Pinterest and BlogSpot. Her video podcast is hosted by iTunes.

www.nataliebuskethomas.com

www.ingramcontent.com/pod-product-compliance
Lightning Source LLC
Chambersburg PA
CBHW062028170626
46813CB00001B/334